DANGER
IN
HIGH HEELS

a High Heels mystery

GEMMA HALLIDAY

For my littlest man, Zac.

CHAPTER ONE

————

The sun was shining, the birds were chirping, the traffic was even flowing on the 405, and I was out of the house enjoying an afternoon cocktail on the patio of a trendy Melrose restaurant with an old friend. Life was good.

"So, where was I?" I asked, momentarily distracted by the overwhelming goodness of my life. (And possibly the effects of the cocktail.)

"I haven't the foggiest," my companion remarked dryly, his British accent lilting across the table to me.

"Right. Livvie," I said, remembering my train of thought. "I swear it was just the cutest thing I have ever seen in my entire life. She and Max were outside, and we'd propped them up with their Boppy pillows, and Max had his binkie on his belly, and Livvie just reached out and got hold of it with her chubby little fists and..." I paused, stealing a glance across the table at my companion. He was smirking at me, raising one eyebrow in an is-this-chick-for-real? expression.

I bit my lip.

"Sorry. I'm doing too much baby talk, aren't I?" I asked.

The smirk turned into a full-fledged grin as he sipped his martini. "Maybe just a smidge."

Recently I'd stumbled across a very odd phenomenon. Not everyone in the world thought my twin babies were as fascinating as I did. Crazy, right? But I'd found that when I was telling the story of how my three-month-old daughter, Olivia, or Livvie as we'd taken to calling her, was spitting up on her car seat or how my son, Max, exactly three minutes younger than his sister, was prone to colic, my fashionably single friends all seemed to yawn, roll their eyes, or smirk (as was the current case) and suddenly remember some very important appointment they were late for. Go figure.

I sighed, reaching for my pomegranate margarita. "Point taken," I mumbled. "Honestly, I swear I can carry on an adult conversation, too."

He waved me off. "Not at all, love. Your Boppy, binkie, boopie-whatever little munchkins sound delightful."

"They are. You know, you really should come see them sometime."

"Uh-huh," he said. "I will. As soon as they stop drooling and leaking from their back ends."

My turn to smirk. Felix Dunn was not what I'd call a baby-person. I'm sure he didn't actually hate them. And he had probably even been one once. But I had a hard time picturing him in the vicinity of one now.

Felix was the managing editor of the *L.A. Informer*, Hollywood's most notorious tabloid, making him much more comfortable stalking an A-lister down the Sunset Strip than holding an infant that may "leak" at any moment. I'd met Felix years ago when we'd both ended up in Las Vegas tracking down a group of Prada smuggling drag queens. Clearly that had been in my pre-husband-and-kids lifetime. But Felix's life was, as far as I could tell, pretty much the same as it had been back then.

Felix was not overly tall, but not what you'd call short either. He had a slim build, sandy blond hair, and blue eyes that always seemed to be twinkling beneath his sandy brows with some sort of secret knowledge. He was dressed today in his usual uniform of a button down shirt and khaki pants, though I noticed that since he'd been promoted from reporter to editor, he'd traded in his sneakers for a respectable pair of oxfords. John Varvatos, if I wasn't mistaken. A splurge I was surprised at, considering Felix's usual tendency toward thriftiness.

"Okay, Dunn," I conceded, "I've got a moratorium on the baby talk. So what was it you wanted to discuss this afternoon?" I asked, switching gears.

Two days ago, Felix had called me out of the blue and asked if I could meet him for lunch. Not that I didn't appreciate the afternoon out, but, as I mentioned, Felix wasn't known for his extravagant generosity in the cash department. If he'd agreed to pay for lunch, I knew he had an agenda.

"Right." He leaned his elbows on the table, studiously avoiding getting any marinara sauce from his pasta dish on his sleeves. "I need your help with a story we're working on. Specifically, I was hoping you could give me some background information on someone."

I raised an eyebrow his way. "Sounds intriguing."

"Lana Paulson. She's in fashion. You know her, correct?" Felix asked.

I nodded, the name jogging an old memory. "Sure. She and I went to design school together. She was my roommate. But that was forever ago." And, at the risk of dating myself unnecessarily, I wasn't going to admit to Felix just how long ago "forever" was. In school Lana'd had a flair for the dramatic, and after graduation she'd taken her talents to Hollywood, designing costumes. I, on the other hand, had gone the footwear route and started my own line of high heeled shoes. "Last I heard Lana had a boutique on Melrose and was wardrobe assistant at some TV network," I told Felix.

He nodded. "Actually, she's the head of wardrobe for UBN now."

"Wow. Good for her," I said, honestly meaning it as I sipped my drink again.

"Anyway," he continued. "One of my reporters recently got a tip that some wardrobe items have gone missing from one of the network's shows."

"Missing?" I asked.

"Stolen," he clarified.

"Exciting. Your paper must be thrilled."

Felix grinned. "Trust me, I am. This is a major story." He paused. "If it's true."

"Ah. So, you want to know if Lana can be trusted."

Felix nodded. "Exactly. Is this a case of an overworked wardrobe woman being careless or an actual crime?"

"Okay, tell me about the theft."

"Well," Felix said, leaning back in his seat again. "The source claims that three separate times now costume items have gone missing. Last, it was the lead's outfit, and the whole production had to shut down. Cost them a day's worth of shooting time, and Lana was in some very hot water with the execs. Time is money."

"So you think maybe she's just claiming theft to cover her ass?" I asked, reading between Felix's cynical lines.

Felix shrugged noncommittally. "What do you think?"

I leaned back in my chair, letting the warm sun wash over my shoulders. "That's a tough one. Like I said, it's been years since I've seen her. Was she a little dramatic? Sure. But this is Hollywood. That's kind of a given."

Felix pursed his lips together, clearly not hearing the answer he was looking for.

"But," I added, "she was good at what she did. Fashion was her life. I couldn't see her simply misplacing something that important. If it were up to me, I'd be inclined to believe your source."

Felix nodded. "Perfect." I could see juicy headlines dancing in his eyes.

I grinned at him. "Since when are you tabloid boys so concerned with the truth, anyway? Don't I seem to remember a time when you pasted my head on the body of Pamela Anderson to pump up one of your stories?"

Felix narrowed his eyes at me. "You're never going to let me live that one down are you?"

I shook my head, feeling my blonde hair whip at my cheeks. "Nope. Not in this lifetime."

"Truth is, those were different times. B.T. Before Twitter," he clarified. "Now, we print something that isn't on the up and up, and everyone and their mother is online calling us liars, propagandists, you name it. Subscribers are a lot more savvy." He paused. "Or possibly just cranky. Either way, we have to be a bit more careful about checking our facts if we don't want to lose followers."

"Well, hurray for Twitter. I'll be expecting a retraction to print any day now," I said, signaling the server for another drink. Hey, I wasn't driving home, Felix was paying, and it was the first time since the twins had been born that I'd left the house without a diaper bag. I was going to enjoy my adult afternoon to the fullest. "So, how are we going to catch the thief?" I asked.

"You want me to talk with Lana? Go undercover on her show? Ferret out some suspects among the cast?"

Felix gave me a funny look over the rim of his martini glass. "Maddie, love, you're a mum now. I wouldn't ask you to do any of those things."

I paused. "But didn't you just say you needed my help?"

"Your background on Lana is plenty enough help," he assured me.

"It is?" I asked, feeling a tiny prickle of disappointment.

"More than enough," he added. "Besides, I've got Allie on the story, and I'm sure if there is a thief at the network, she'll get to the bottom of it."

I felt a frown marring my perfect afternoon out.

Allie Quick was one of Felix's star reporters on the *Informer* staff. She also just happened to be his girlfriend, ten years his junior, and the living embodiment of Barbie. While my first impression had been dumb-blonde all the way, she'd actually proven to be a good reporter, so I had to give her credit there. However, I suddenly had the faintest feeling of being replaced by a younger model.

"But what does Allie know about fashion?" I protested. "I mean, I could at least have lunch with Lana. Get the details for you."

Again Felix shook his head, closing his blue eyes and doing a frown-slash-smile thing that had "patronizing" written all over it. "Don't worry a bit about it, Maddie. Allie's got it under control. In fact, she's meeting Lana this evening at her boutique to get the full story."

"Hmm. Well, tell her to say 'hi' to Lana for me," I mumbled.

Felix nodded. "Will do. But don't worry, love. Really, we've got this one. You just go home and enjoy your drooling monsters. Leave the heavy lifting to those of us not graced with the joys of motherhood."

CHAPTER TWO

An hour later Felix had dropped me off outside the nineteen-fifties style bungalow I shared with my husband and two kids. My babysitter's, A.K.A. Mom's, car was parked in the drive, and I could already hear shouts of teeny tiny protests from beyond the front door as I walked up the slate pathway.

Even though I loved my twins with all my heart, I paused just a moment before opening the door, enjoying my last breath of freedom before I pushed inside the house. Where I was immediately assaulted with wails (from the twins), baby-talk (from mom), and a loud sigh (probably from me).

"Mommy's home," I announced from the doorway, dropping my purse on the floor and kicking off the kitten heels I'd worn to lunch.

"Perfect timing, Mads," Mom called out, emerging from the twins' bedroom with a screaming bundle swaddled in a pink blanket. With a pink body suit on. And pink booties. And a pink, wool hat. I prayed it was Livvie.

"I think they're hungry," she said.

"Mom, you do know that it's eighty-five degrees out, right?" I asked, taking the baby from her and peeking beneath the layers. Thankfully we had a female.

"But it's winter," Mom protested.

"We live in L.A. Winter means T-shirts instead of tank tops."

Mom shook her head at me. "Babies need to be kept warm," she said, picking up an almost identical blue bundle from the play mat in the corner of the living room.

"Warm, yes. Cooked, no," I protested, removing Livvie's hat to expose a soft dusting of blonde peach fuzz along her scalp.

But Mom waved me off. "I'll get the bottles, you hold," she commanded, shoving the blue bundle into my arms as well.

Luckily, both babies were fabulous eaters (I had no idea where they got that trait. Couldn't have had anything to do with the nightly tubs of Ben & Jerry's I'd ingested while pregnant.), and as soon as we'd settled them in their respective carriers with their little bottles of milk, they were both happy as clams, the roars of tiny screams ceasing. After a good six ounces a piece, a pair of burps loud enough to make their father proud, and two wet diaper changes, they both settled into blissful newborn happiness, cooing at each other on the play mat again.

"Okay, I'm off," Mom announced, wrapping a polyester scarf around her neck and grabbing her purse. "There's a sale today at Sears, and Dorothy and I both have coupons."

I cringed. As much as I loved my mother, the one thing in this world that I was most thankful for was that I had not inherited her sense of style. Somehow her fashion sense had peaked around 1989 and stayed there ever since. Today she was clad in a pair of acid washed jeans that were at least two sizes too big in the rear, white Keds that looked as if they'd been bedazzled with pink rhinestones along the top, and a bright green sweater with a kitten chasing a ball of yarn on the front of it. With matching green eye shadow that went clear up to her eyebrows. Sadly, I was not surprised she was buying clothes at a store that sold power tools.

"You know, I have a gift card for Nordstrom, Mom. I'd be happy to take you shopping there any time," I offered, trying to steer her in the right direction.

But Mom waved me off. "Nonsense. That stuff is way too overpriced. Take these jeans for instance. You know what I paid for these?"

I looked down at their pale denim glory. Whatever it was, it was way too much.

"$14.99," she said proudly. "What a steal, huh?"

I bit my lip, holding back the slew of snide remarks bubbling up in my throat. She was, after all, my mother.

"You know," Mom said, a scary light bulb look going off in her eyes. "If Dorothy has a couple of extra coupons, I could pick up a pair for you. I think they're still on sale."

"Oh, gee, wow. That would be...yeah, you know I think I'm good on jeans right now."

"It would be no trouble."

"I'm...still trying to lose baby weight. Not a good time to buy new clothes."

"But you have to wear something."

"I'm good. Honest."

"You sure?"

"I have never been more sure of anything in my life."

Mom shrugged, slipping on a leopard print jacket. "Okay, suit yourself. But if you change your mind, just send me a text," she said, pointing to her cell. Texting was Mom's latest thing. Her husband had finally convinced her to join this century and bought her a smart phone for her birthday. Fifteen times a day I got little notes telling me she was "loling @ ur stepdad" or "h8ing the new amricn idol jdg".

"Will do," I promised. And thanks for watching the kids," I added as she stepped out.

"Any time, Maddie," she called over her shoulder before shutting the door.

Whew, close one.

I left the twins to their happy babbling while I changed the laundry, put away a load of clean dishes, and checked my email. Basically doing the frantic mad-dash that had become my everyday holy-crap-no-one's-crying-quick-get-something-done routine. It lasted the average fifteen minutes before a foul smell came from Livvie's corner, and Max started protesting in shrill, ear-drum splitting cries. I'd swear the child was destined to become a lead singer of a heavy metal band.

I was just cleaning up Livvie's mess and pleading with Max to stop yelling, when a text vibrated from my pocket. I did a silent prayer that it wasn't from my Mom saying she'd found acid wash in my size. I put Livvie down, swapping her for her brother, then checked the readout. It was from my husband.

Homicide just came in. Gotta stay late. Sorry. XOXO

I sighed. (Though the sound was swallowed up by Max's howls.) My husband was detective Jack Ramirez, L.A.P.D. Homicide. And, while we had both agreed that I, and not my husband, would be the one taking a hiatus from work when the twins arrived, I hadn't realized at the time that it meant I'd basically be a single mom most nights. Not that it was his fault. A notoriously unpredictable work schedule kinda came with the territory. I mean, it was hard to convince people to get killed just between the hours of nine and five.

I looked down at the twins. "Well, I guess it's just you and me again tonight, noisemakers."

* * *

The next morning found the twins in a much better mood, my husband gone again before dawn, and me sipping a cup of very strong coffee across the living room floor from my best friend, Dana.

"You didn't sleep again last night, did you?" Dana asked, stealing a glance at me over the rim of her coffee cup. Organic with soy milk and Stevia sweetener.

"Does it show?" I responded, checking my eyes for lower lid bags in the fun-house style mirror attached to the twins' play mat.

"Just a little," Dana said. "But I have some concealer samples that will do wonders."

I sipped at my coffee (non-fat, no-calorie sweetener, sugar-free vanilla syrup) while I watched Dana dig into her purse.

I first met Dana Dashel when we'd both attended John Adams Middle School in Reseda. She'd been the only other girl in seventh grade who understood the power of tasteful eye make-up. Her hair was a light strawberry blonde, her eyes a bright blue, and she was at least five inches taller than I was, bringing her within a breath of supermodel height. And her addiction to the gym was almost as strong as my addiction to junk food. (Or maybe I should say my pre-baby-weight addiction to junk food. I was currently at three months sugar-free and hating every minute of my glucose sobriety.)

Dana was an actress who, in addition to landing several hot supporting roles lately, was the face of the Lover Girl cosmetics commercials. Which meant she always had free samples.

I gratefully took the proffered concealer, applying a generous helping in the baby mirror.

"Last night wasn't as bad as some," I told her. "I did get a solid three hour stretch at one point."

"You should get out of the house," Dana told me. "Maybe some fresh air would wear them out."

"Fresh air like at the mall?" I asked, warming to the idea.

"Actually, I was thinking of visiting Ricky on set."

Ricky Montgomery was Dana's boyfriend, a movie star, and had abs you could do laundry on. He and Dana were rivaling George Clooney and whatshername as the top celebrity couple in TMZ's latest polls. Ricky's current gig was on a reality show called *Dancing with Celebrities*. Ten celebrities from various walks of Hollywood life paired up with professional ballroom dancers to compete for the ultimate title of Celebrity Dance Champion. Each week they engaged in tricky tangos and wild waltzes for the viewing public, who then voted off their least favorite dancer/celebrity combo. They were only in week three of live competitions, but so far Ricky and his partner, Irina Sokolov, had been fan favorites. Not surprising since the show's demographic was mostly female, and Ricky was currently being touted as "Hollywood's most eligible bachelor" (according to *People*). Possibly one reason Dana was a frequent visitor on the set.

"I wish I could," I said, sincerely meaning it. The costumes looked to die for on TV; I could only imagine the fabulosity in person. "But I'm not sure they'd be welcome," I added, gesturing to the pudgy pair of babies currently blowing raspberries at each other.

"Are you kidding? They're so cute, I'm sure no one would mind them."

"Right, no one would mind me bringing a pair of screaming infants to a closed set. And their huge diaper bag. And their milk, their changing pads, their playmobiles, their-"

"Okay, okay, I get the point," Dana said holding her hands up.

"Sorry, but I'm kinda homebound at the moment," I said, sipping my coffee again.

Dana sighed, letting Max grab her finger with his chubby fist. "I want one of these."

I raised an eyebrow at her. "I'll sell you one cheap."

She grinned, elbowing me in the ribs. "No, I'm serious. I mean, I've always thought of myself as the motherly type."

I raised the other eyebrow. "Really?" Honestly this was the first I'd heard of it. Dana had always been more of the film-opening type than the diaper-genie type.

"Well, okay, maybe not *always*," she admitted, "but I can feel it ticking, you know. The 'biological clock,'" she said, rolling her eyes and doing air quotes. "I have a bad feeling its alarm may go off soon."

I shook my head. "Honey, you have plenty of time." Dana was my age. I refused to think of any clock running out on either of us anytime soon.

But Dana shook her head. "No. I don't. Not really. I mean, even if Ricky were to pop the question today, we'd need at least eighteen months to plan the wedding, then we'd want to go on an extended honeymoon, and we always said we'd like to travel a little before bringing kids into the picture, so we're looking at three years down the line before I even get pregnant. Then another nine months on top of that, and if we want him to have a sibling that could be another two years before baby number two comes along and then... boom! Too late. Hot flash city and I'm all barren."

I blinked at her. "Wow. You've really thought this through."

Dana sighed. "Well, I've had a lot of time to think about it. You realize that Ricky and I have been dating for almost three years now, and he's not so much as breathed a whisper of a ring."

"I'm sorry," I said, laying a hand on her arm. "I didn't realize it's been that long."

"It has." She tickled Max under his chin, resulting in a smile full of spit bubbles. "At this rate, I may never get one of these."

"Well, listen, you are free to borrow mine any time you like."

She smiled. "Thanks."

"Hey, doesn't *Dancing with Celebrities* air on UBN?" I asked Dana, trying to steer the conversation back to more comfortable subjects than barrenness and blaring biological alarm clocks.

Dana nodded. "Yeah. Why?"

"Well, I just saw Felix yesterday..."

Dana raised an eyebrow at me. "Tabloid Boy? What's he up to?"

"The usual. He wanted to know about a schoolmate of mine who is working wardrobe for the network. He has a source who says someone is stealing clothes."

"Ooooo, naughty. So, what did he want you to do? Go undercover? Investigate?" She asked.

I frowned. "No. That's just it. He just wanted to know about her character. He didn't want me to *do* anything."

Dana scrunched up her nose. "Why not? You're like totally good at finding things out."

"I know, right?" I agreed. "He's got Allie Quick on it instead."

Dana scrunched her forehead up to match her nose, making a face that would produce Botox-proof wrinkles if she wasn't careful. "You're way better at investigating than Allie."

I shot her a grateful look. "Thanks."

"Hey, you know what?" she said.

I bit. "What?"

"I bet Ricky could get us into wardrobe at UBN with no problem."

"Really?" I asked.

"Sure. I mean, he's there all the time. I bet he totally has access."

I sucked in the side of my cheek. What harm would there be in just visiting the set, checking out the wardrobe department, and chatting with an old friend?

"Ricky wouldn't mind?" I asked. "I mean, I don't want to cut into his rehearsal time."

Dana waved me off. "Are you kidding? He's usually dying for an excuse to take a break. That Irina is a slave driver."

I pursed my lips. In that case, it was almost irresponsible of me *not* to look into Felix's theft story. I sort of even owed it to Felix to help him out, right? I mean, I'm sure if I thought hard enough I could think of a time in the past when he'd helped me out. At the very least, he'd bought me two pomegranate margs at lunch. I really should return the favor.

"An insider's view *is* something that Allie would never be able to get," I mused out loud, knowing that the network had a strict no-paparazzi policy. It did not, on the other hand, have a no-friends-of-the-girlfriends-of-its-stars policy.

Dana nodded. "Totally. We'd be way inside."

I looked down at the twins gurgling a little spit bubble symphony. "You know, if we could get them to nap in the car, maybe they'd be quiet on set after all."

CHAPTER THREE

Only a scant forty-five minutes later I had the diaper bag packed, the bottles made, the extra outfits picked out and shoved into the bottom of my purse, baby toys, baby wipes, baby blankets, and two clean, semi-happy children strapped into car seats in the back of my Honda Odyssey.

Yes, it's true. I now drove a minivan. With a "Baby on Board" sign suctioned to the back window. Commence laughing at me.

When I'd first found out I was pregnant, I'd been hesitant about the ability of my little red Jeep to hold my new precious cargo. Sure it was awesome for buzzing around town with the top down on a sunny day, but it wasn't exactly the quintessential mom-mobile. But when I'd found out I was not having just one, but two little bundles of joy, I knew I was going to need a new car. I had resisted the minivan at first, looking at every four-door sedan and SUV on the market. But the truth was, the minivan was so easy. The doors opened on their own, the seats were big enough for two car seats plus all the baby gear, and there was even a built in TV in the back of each headrest for when the kids got old enough to stare at Elmo. So, I'd relented. Hanging my head in shame, I had bought a minivan.

But I hadn't been able to completely let go of my first baby - my Jeep. It was still tucked away in the garage, just waiting for a time when a top-down, carefree day might come my way again. (Even if that didn't look likely for at least another eighteen years.)

Thankfully the twins didn't mind car rides and did, in fact, sleep most of the way to the UBN Studios. Dana gave her name to the guard at the gates, which, of course, was on the list, and we were quickly ushered into a lot to our right where we parked and pulled out the twins' huge double stroller, ever so carefully attaching their car seats to the top to keep them asleep as we transferred them.

The United Broadcasting Network was a fairly new network, cropping up on basic cable and vying for valuable Nielsen airtime with the big boys of NBC, CBS, and ABC. They started out filling the prime-time sitcom void with fresh premises and out-of-the-box humor, then graduated to the mother lode of ratings grabbers with a string of reality shows. They had a show about an aging rock star's crazy teenage kids, a weight loss show featuring flab to fab results of former child stars, and, of course, *Dancing with Celebrities*, which, thanks to featuring an eclectic cast including a Teen Mom whose fifteen minutes of fame should have ended hours ago, a former NFL player turned tranny, and heart-throb Ricky, this season had launched the network into the front-runner of the ratings race. Personally, I was addicted and voted for Ricky every week.

The network studios themselves looked shockingly like any other office building complex in Los Angeles. Squat, stucco buildings with brown clay-tiled roofs were arranged around a central courtyard with a bubbling fountain and tasteful landscaping. Behind the offices sat a row of warehouses that housed sets for the various TV shows currently shooting. Interspersed between the warehouses were white trailers, holding mobile wardrobe racks, props, and designer coffee drinks. Dana and I pushed the monster stroller down an alleyway lined with white trailers stopping at studio 3B, where a bright orange sign above the door proclaimed it was home to *Dancing with Celebrities.*

Dana and I walked through the large doors that reminded me of the ones on our garage at home, immediately assaulted by the sounds of the rumba being blasted at top volume. The cameras were absent today, but a dozen guys in cargo shorts and T-shirts reading "crew" laid cables, arranged microphones, and adjusted lights, getting positions ready to capture the dance from all angles once they went live. To our right sat a set of bleachers, empty now but ready to hold the live studio audience once shooting began on Wednesday. To the left was a bandstand, though the rumba we currently heard was not being shouted out by a live horn section but by speakers hidden in the ceiling somewhere. And in the center of the room was a polished, hardwood stage, bathed in bright spotlights, where Ricky and Irina were dancing their hearts out in sparkly, sequined outfits. Ricky's was a tuxedo style pantsuit, and Irina's a skin-tight, red dress that ended just below her butt.

Dana took one look at the barely-there skirt, and a frown settled between her brows. Her jaw clenched, and her lips set in a grim, tight line, jealousy radiating off of her.

I put a hand on her arm in a show of support as I watched Ricky and Irina finish their rumba, seriously impressed at Ricky's moves. While the sweat on his forehead indicated that he was working hard to keep up with Irina, the fact that just two months ago he'd never even heard of the rumba, let alone attempted the ballroom dance, was pretty amazing. I had a feeling he might even be in the running to win the whole competition.

The music finally ended with Ricky and Irina striking a stunning pose as he held her high off the dance floor. As soon as he set her down, Ricky spotted us and sauntered over, pausing only long enough to grab a water bottle from the Craft Service table.

"Hey, babe," he said, coming in to give Dana a kiss.

"Eww, you're all sweaty," she giggled, though I noticed she didn't move away as his lips hit her cheek.

"What are you ladies doing here?" he asked.

"Oh, we just thought you could use a visit," Dana replied.

He grinned at her. "You just can't stay away, can you?"

"You know you love the attention," she teased.

His grinned widened as he looked past her. "And I see you brought babies with you."

"Don't worry," I quickly reassured him. "I'm outta here if they start screaming."

Ricky waved me off. "Who, these little guys? I can't imagine them causing any trouble," he said. Though, he did look slightly relieved. "So what do you think of my rumba?" he asked, gesturing to the dance floor.

"Awesome!" I said, the fan girl in me coming out. "Ohmigod, you and Irina are amazing together."

Dana's tight frown returned.

"I mean, you dance amazingly together," I quickly backpedaled.

"Thanks," Ricky said, chugging his water. "I swear the football workouts I did in high school were nowhere near this hard. These dancer chicks are hard core."

As much as I was enjoying talking dance, I knew I was on borrowed time before the munchkins started screaming again. I figured I'd better get to the point of the visit.

"Hey, do you happen to know where wardrobe is?" I asked.

Ricky shrugged. "For which show?"

Good question. "Actually, I'm looking for Lana Paulson. She's head of wardrobe for the network."

Recognition dawned in Ricky's eyes. "Sure. She's in the big, white building at the back of the lot."

"Awesome." I paused. "Do you happen to know her?" I asked.

He nodded. "She does all our costumes."

I cocked my head to the side. "I would have thought she had assistants doing the actual costuming."

"She does," he agreed. "For most shows. But DWC is like the granddaddy of costume shows, you know? She said she's waited her whole life for a gig like this."

I suddenly felt bad for her. If she had waited her whole life, then someone was stealing her creations and ruining that one chance, she was in trouble.

"There's a rumor going around that someone is stealing items from her," I told him.

Ricky paused a moment, biting the inside of his cheek. "That would explain a lot."

"Explain what?" I asked, jumping on the phrase.

"Well, last week they had to shut down production for a day," he said, echoing the story Felix had told me. "We were supposed to be doing a dress rehearsal, and Lana couldn't find the sequined gown Shaniqua was supposed to wear for her tango."

"Shaniqua – the football player turned..." I paused, searching for the appropriately PC term.

"Turned chick," Ricky supplied for me, clearly not as concerned with PC as I was. "She used to be Shawn Jones. She's actually really cool. I'd offer to introduce you, but she's rehearsing next door right now."

"So, the gown. It was stolen?" I asked.

He shook his head. "No, just misplaced. But the director was pissed. He was shouting at Lana so loudly she was crying. I kinda felt bad for her. I mean, we all misplace stuff sometimes, you know?"

"So it *wasn't* stolen?" I asked. I'll admit it, stolen gowns were the most excitement I'd seen in months. I was kind of disappointed to see it slipping away as nothing more than an absentminded wardrobe woman trying to save her job.

"No. She did eventually find it. It was stuck in the wrong wardrobe rack. We all just figured she forgot where she put it."

"What about the other items?" I asked him. "I heard there were two other items missing before the gown. Were they ever found?"

Ricky shrugged. "Sorry. This is the first I've heard of it. You'd have to ask Lana, I guess."

"Any idea who has access to wardrobe?" I asked.

Ricky squinted past me. "Well, it's housed in the wardrobe building overnight and locked up pretty tight. But during the day, they bring it all on set. Some goes in our dressing rooms, some stays in the trailer. It's honestly all over. Anyone could grab an item unnoticed, really."

Which was good and bad for Felix's story. It proved that theft was *possible*, but it didn't narrow down a field of suspects any.

"Ricky, Irina's ready to go over the footwork again," a guy in a black crew shirt yelled from across the room.

"Sorry. Duty calls," Ricky said. Then he gave Dana a quick peck on the cheek before running over to stand in the spotlight. Irina appeared again on set to join him, lifting her head high, elongating her dancer's neck, as she took Ricky's hands in hers, standing frozen in their first pose as they waited for the music to start.

Max stirred in his stroller, and I held my breath, hoping he'd keep quiet long enough to watch. I did some stroller jiggling as the music started.

Irina snapped to attention, concentration taut in her face as she arched her body around Ricky's.

I stole a quick glance at Dana. Her mouth was set in that grim line again, her eyes narrowed, her jaw clenched. Poor thing. We were only three episodes in. She had a lot of watching her man dance with someone else ahead of her.

The rumba was over surprisingly quickly, ending in the same air-lifted pose we'd seen before. As soon as the music stopped and Ricky placed his partner back on the floor, Irina's face broke into a frown.

"Too slow," she said, a thick accent coloring her speech. "We'll do it again."

Ricky sighed. "We've done it four times."

"We'll do it until you have it right!" she snapped, then turned on heel and walked back offstage again, down a hall leading to the left. "Re-set the music," I heard her yell as she disappeared.

Ricky turned Dana's way, sent her a grin, then rolled his eyes before grabbing his water bottle.

And in the carriage, Max started squirming and making little mewing sounds.

"I think I better go feed the animals," I reluctantly told Dana.

She nodded, her face relaxing in direct proportion to the distance now between Ricky and his hot co-star. "Sure. There's a lounge just behind the bleachers. It's usually empty."

I nodded. "You coming with?"

She shook her head. "If you don't need me, I think I'm going to stay and watch them practice."

Which I interpreted to mean she didn't want to leave Irina and her man alone.

"'K. Be back in a sec," I promised, popping the brakes up on the stroller and heading toward the lounge.

I found it easily enough, a plain, square room filled with non-descript sofas, a microwave, and a water cooler. Again, it reminded me of an office building much more than the glamour of Hollywood. I plopped myself down in one of the chairs, then grabbed the bottles from the diaper bag and mixed their powdery stuff with some bottled water.

While I'd honestly tried to breast feed at first, I'd learned very quickly that with twins, that meant ninety percent of the time I had a small person attached to my chest. Kinda made it hard to do anything but make milk. By week two I'd felt so much like a cow that the wheat grass juice Dana drank daily was starting to look appetizing. I'd made the wise decision to switch to pumping half time, and going formula half time. Honestly, the twins seemed just as content with a baby bottle in their mouths, and I was *way* more content. And less prone to grass cravings.

After a couple of suck downs and a quick burp on the back for each, we were once again settled into the carriage. I pushed the little ones out onto the set, hoping to grab Dana and go track down Lana.

But as soon as I turned the corner, I realized something much bigger than wardrobe malfunctions was going on.

The stage was abandoned, grips and PA's were running in every direction shouting into their walkie-talkies. A new addition of about half a dozen security guards was swarming the set. And dancers in sweats and tiny T-shirts were waving their arms and shouting loudly enough that even if the twins hadn't been fat and happy at the moment, they would have been totally drowned out.

I pushed the stroller down toward the hallway I'd seen before, craning for a glimpse of Dana or Ricky. A group of hair and make-up people were crowded together, talking in hushed tones, shaking their heads.

Anxiety began to rise in my gut. Something about the scene did not feel business-as-usual.

"What's going on?" I asked a girl in an apron loaded with cosmetics.

She whirled around, eyes wide. "They found Irina," she told me.

"Was she missing?" I asked, trying to play catch up. Last I'd seen, she was setting to rehearse again. How long had I been gone feeding the babies? Twenty minutes? Half hour tops?

The girl nodded, her sloppy bun bobbing up and down on top of her head. "When they went to set the music again, no one could find her. She wasn't in her dressing room, or wardrobe, or anywhere."

"But you just said they did finally find her," I reminded her, knowing there was more to the story, or else everyone would be wearing looks of relief, not the frowns of anxiety marking their faces now.

She nodded again. "They found her in Ricky Montgomery's dressing room. Naked," she added.

Oh lord. Dana was going to freak!

But what I heard next made me realize that Dana was the least of the girl's problems.

"She's…" The make-up girl paused, her face paling. "Dead."

CHAPTER FOUR

There are two things that everyone knows about me. One: I live for fashion. As a child I spent more hours than I care to count dressing my dolls for every special occasion under the sun. In fact, I spent so much time dressing my dolls that they never actually attended any special occasions. When I ran out of pre-made doll fashions, I started using whatever I had on hand to create my own. Socks, handkerchiefs, scarves - all were fair game to my pair of safety scissors and glue stick as I cut, wrapped, draped, and stuck the items to my uniquely styled dolls.

As soon as I got to high school, and my dolls went the way of the yard sale, I started experimenting with my own clothes. Very seldom did I buy an outfit off the rack and wear it as-is. Normally my scissors (sharp sewing ones this time) did their magic first, creating one-of-a-kind custom garments. After graduating, I was accepted to the Academy of Art Fashion Design School in San Francisco, where I found my true fashion passion - shoes. No matter how tall you were, how short, how fat, how thin, every woman could fit into a fabulous pair of shoes. I started designing Paris-worthy pumps then and never looked back.

That was the first thing people knew about me. The second thing? I'm ashamed to say I'm a bit of a dead body magnet.

Know how some people have all the luck when it comes to bingo or sweepstakes? I have all the murder luck. I swear I do nothing on my own to incur this sort of luck, but it seems to follow me everywhere I go. My first run-in with death was back when I met Ramirez, and we were tracking down my MIA ex-boyfriend. Since then, I'd had the fortune - or misfortune - of being involved with several of his cases. But to be fair, I'd even helped solve a few.

So while the word "dead" uttered by the make-up girl churned my stomach, I was not altogether as shocked as one might think.

Like a good friend, my first thought was of Dana. She must be hysterical that not only had a dead woman been found, but a *naked* dead woman in her *boyfriend*'s dressing room.

But I'll admit that a close second thought was much more selfish and closer to home. My husband was going to be so pissed. I consoled myself with the fact that I had not *technically* been the one to find the body this time. In fact, I'd been yards away, feeding the babies at the time. So, really, I wasn't even sure you could count this as a Maddie Body at all.

At least, that was the story I was sticking with.

I quickly pointed the gargantuan stroller past the crowd of make-up people (Okay, maybe *quickly* was a slight exaggeration since a stroller that size does not move anywhere quickly.) and down the hallway, off of which were a series of closed doors. One read "Shaniqua", another "Kaylie", which I recognized as the Teen Mom on the show, and the last was labeled "Ricky Montgomery". That one, predictably, had a crowd of people standing around it, including several grips, dancers, and more hair and make-up people. They were all watching the scene with undisguised interest, while a pair of guys in white security shirts and black shorts stood at the door, barring anyone's entry.

I scanned the onlookers for a tall, strawberry blonde. But as it turned out, I heard Dana before I caught a glimpse of her.

"She was doing *what* naked in your dressing room?" Dana shouted.

Uh-oh.

"Babe, you've gotta calm down," I heard Ricky's voice in response.

"I don't gotta do anything, *babe*," Dana yelled back.

"Look, I don't know how she got there," Ricky protested.

"And why was she naked?" Dana asked.

"I don't know!"

"And where were you?" Dana countered.

I stood on tip-toe and caught a glimpse of her. Hands on hips, eyes narrowed into slits, lips pursed. Ears practically spewing steam.

"I... I... I don't know. It was busy, there was a lot going on. You know how it is on set. Everything crazy..." Ricky's voice trailed off unconvincingly.

"Oh my God," Dana yelled, throwing her hands up. "I leave you alone for one minute, and the next thing I know you're screwing your co-star behind my back!"

"I was not!" Ricky protested. "I was just... I mean we were..."

"You were what?" Dana asked, leaning in close and poking him in the chest with one manicured finger. "You were doing what with a *naked* dancer in your dressing room?"

"Look, this isn't really the place to do this," Ricky said, eyes shifting to the growing crowd, no doubt hearing the entire conversation played back in his head through the reporting of paparazzi.

But clearly Dana didn't care. Dana was freaking, and she was not backing down for anything.

"Give me one good reason why I shouldn't tear you limb from limb right now, pal," she said, her voice low, menacing, and filled with the kind of threat that a woman who engages in cardio kickboxing six out of seven days a week can carry through with.

As I leaned in closer, waiting for Ricky's reply, I felt a hand tap me on the shoulder.

"Hey, what's going on?"

"Fight," I said without turning around. "Ricky's so busted."

"Busted for what?" came the reply.

"Cheating on Dana with a dead girl and-" I froze mid-sentence as I turned around to see the speaker.

And came face to face with a tall, dark-haired, broad chested guy. My husband, Detective Jack Ramirez, LAPD Homicide.

I gulped.

Ramirez raised one dark eyebrow at me. "Dead girl?" he asked.

I nodded. Reluctantly. "But I swear I was nowhere near the dressing room when they found her. I was feeding the babies. Waaaaaaay over there," I said, drawing out the word as I pointed back toward the lounge.

Ramirez stuck his hands in his pockets and rocked back on his heels. "'Way' over there, huh?"

"Did you hear the part about how I did not find her?" I emphasized.

"You just can't stay out of trouble, can you, Springer?" he asked, the use of my last name giving me some relief that he wasn't in the livid-pissed range, but more exasperated-pissed.

"I'm guessing this is your case now?" I asked.

He nodded, glancing at the dressing room door. "I presume she's in there?"

"I think so. But," I added, "like I said, I haven't actually even seen the dead body. I'm so out of the loop this time." I held both hands up in an innocent gesture to bring home my point.

He shot me a look. "*This* time."

"Exactly."

He took a deep breath. "Okay." He paused, looking down at the babies gurgling with happy, full stomachs in the stroller. "I'd ask you to go home, but that's not gonna happen, is it?"

I gave him an apologetic look. "Well, I can't just leave Dana here..."

"All right, all right. Tell you what: wait with Dana. But once we get her statement you both go right home. *Capice*?"

I nodded and did a mock salute. "Scout's honor."

Ramirez shot me a look that said he didn't really believe I'd been a scout, let alone was going to keep clear of the murder scene. But he gave me a quick kiss on the cheek before pulling out his badge and pushing his way toward Ricky's dressing room.

Fifteen minutes later, Ramirez's entire crew of backup arrived, including CSU in black jackets carrying rolls of crime scene tape, a coroner with a stretcher, and a bunch of guys in uniforms who spread out to question people like a well-organized army.

Dana and I sat on the bleachers, watching the scene unfold almost as if we were the audience witnessing a crime drama play out. Only as we watched two guys in plainclothes question Ricky, it hit home how very real this all was.

Ricky gestured wildly with his arms as the first guy tried to calm him down (obviously Good Cop) and the second gave him a hard stare (clearly Bad Cop).

I felt my phone buzz in my pocket and pulled it out to see a text from my mom.

omg. dead grl in rm's dressin room?

I cringed. "Looks like the media has already gotten hold of this story." I showed Dana the text.

She did a mirror image of my cringe. "Fab."

true, I texted back to Mom. *Where did u c the story?*

informer website, she typed back.

I whipped my head around, half expecting to see the perky blonde head of Allie Quick bobbing through the crowd. It took me a second to remember, duh, no press were allowed on set. Which meant Allie must have an informant on the set. I scanned the assembled grips, PA's, dancers, celebrities and various other scattered crew, wondering just which one of them was feeding her info.

"I missed the end of your fight," I told Dana, as I tucked my phone back in my pocket. "I'm guessing Ricky had no explanation for Irina being in his dressing room."

"*Nude* in his dressing room," she added. Then shook her head, her face a blank as she watched Ricky. "And, no. Three years. You spend that kind of time with someone, and you think you know them."

"You really think he was cheating on you?" I asked.

Dana blew out a big breath. "I don't know what to believe."

"How long did you leave him alone?" I asked.

"Just a few minutes," Dana said. "Or, I don't know. Maybe a little longer, I guess. I got a call from my agent about the Lover Girl shoot next week. I stepped outside to take it, and when I came back in, everyone was looking for Irina. It wasn't until they found her that I saw Ricky again."

"I hate to be the one to point this out," I said, watching as Bad Cop took his turn grilling Ricky, "but it really doesn't look good that she was found in Ricky's dressing room."

"I know. I know. I mean, what else would she be doing there au naturel, right?"

I shifted uncomfortably on the bleachers. "No, I mean... well... I didn't exactly hear an iron clad alibi back there when you asked where he was earlier?"

Her eyes went big and round. "Oh, no. No way. Ricky did *not* kill that girl. I mean, there's a big difference between cheating and killing."

I nodded. "I know. But I'm just saying it doesn't look good. To the cops. Or the press," I added, gesturing to my phone. "Or anyone else."

Dana turned to watch Ricky again. "He needs a lawyer, doesn't he?" she asked.

I nodded. "If I were in his shoes? I'd want one."

"This is such a nightmare."

"Sorry," I said, rubbing her shoulders.

Just then Livvie started whining and squirming in her seat. I picked her up, and a certain odor wafted up to my nostrils.

"Uh-oh. Nature calls."

"Go ahead," Dana waved at me. "I'll be fine."

"I'll be right back," I assured her, turning the stroller in the direction of the lounge again.

Dana nodded, her eyes still on Ricky. "God, the *Informer* is going to crucify him, aren't they?"

I bit my lip. I had a bad feeling that if Bad Cop's scowl was any indication, the media was going to be the least of Ricky's problems.

* * *

Predictably, it was late when Ramirez finally got home that night. I'd already dropped Dana off at home, fed the babies again, microwaved a Lean Cuisine for myself (baby weight, thou art my mortal enemy!), and put the little ones down for the night, settling myself in front of a DVR-ed episode of *Project Runway* by the time he made an appearance at the front door.

He looked tired, hungry, and like he needed a hug. I started with the third one.

"Long day at the office?" I asked when I finally broke the embrace.

He grinned down at me. "You could say that. Ever take the statements of nine different media-hungry celebrities in one day? I swear they gave the term 'drama queen' new meaning."

I couldn't help but smile. "There's a cold six-pack in the fridge."

Ramirez raised an eyebrow at me. "You're not trying to butter me up for something are you?"

"Who me?" I asked, blinking innocently. "Of course not. I just thought you might like a cool drink while you tell me what happened to Irina today."

Ramirez paused, one hand on the refrigerator door. "Uh-huh. I knew the six-pack came with a price."

"Oh, come on." I swatted him on the shoulder. "She was found in Ricky's dressing room. That's my friend we're talking about. You can't keep me in the dark."

Ramirez twisted the top off a bottle of beer and took a long swallow before answering. "Okay. I can tell you the basics."

I leaned my elbows on the kitchen counter, giving him my full attention. "How did she die?" I asked.

"Subdural hematoma."

"Bump on the head?" I asked, translating.

He nodded. "A big one." He paused, examining the refrigerator contents. "You eaten?"

"I had a Lean Cuisine."

"So, that's a no?"

I shot him a look. "Unless you want a wife with a butt the size of the Hollywood Bowl, you're on your own for dinner."

He stole a glance at my back end. "Looks good to me."

"You," I responded, reaching up on my tip-toes to kiss him on the cheek, "are a very wise man. But you're still on your own for dinner."

He shrugged, grabbing some lunch meat and a jar of pickles.

"So, someone hit Irina on the head hard enough to kill her," I said, steering the conversation back on track.

Ramirez nodded. "Uh-huh. Back of the head. She would have been out cold instantly. Probably never even saw it coming." He grabbed a pickle from the jar and munched down on it.

"Hit with what?" I asked.

Ramirez shrugged. "M.E. hasn't determined the murder weapon yet. Nothing obvious was left at the scene."

"So the murderer took the weapon with him," I mused out loud.

Ramirez paused, pickle dangling in mid air. "Oh, no."

"What?"

"No way, Springer. I know that look in your eyes."

"What? What look?" I asked innocently, stealing a sip of his beer to cover any unwanted "look".

"The 'I'm thinking about sticking my nose in my husband's murder case' look. Not this time. You're supposed to be on maternity leave, being a stay-at-home mom, enjoying our babies, and relaxing."

I shot him a look. "Relaxing? Seriously? Have you met our children? I think it's been three months since I've peed alone."

He grinned. "But they're cute, aren't they?"

"Very," I agreed. "And worth every sleepless, demanding moment, which is why I'm going to ignore the sexist undertones in their father's statement. However, what about Ricky?"

"What about him?"

"Those cops were looking at him like he was a suspect."

"Look, leave Ricky's well-being to me."

I narrowed my eyes. "So you'll make sure they know that Ricky did not kill that girl?"

"I will make sure that all evidence is processed, all leads are followed, and the guilty party goes to jail."

"You didn't mention Ricky's innocence in there."

"No. I didn't." He grabbed a couple slices of ham and tossed them into his mouth.

"You don't think he actually had anything to do with this, do you?" I asked.

"Off the record?" he asked, around his mouthful. "No. But I wouldn't be doing my job if I let personal feelings interfere with an investigation."

"Hmm," I responded, crossing my arms over my chest.

Ramirez paused again. "I give. What does 'Hmm' mean?"

I shrugged. "Nothing."

"Maddie..."

"Nothing. I trust you to do your job."

He narrowed his eyes at me. "Hmm," he said, mimicking my unconvincing sound.

I grinned and couldn't help leaning in for a kiss. "You're cute when you're trying to be all stern and commanding."

Ramirez shook his head at me, though I could tell my "cute" comment softened the look in his eyes some. "Leave this one alone, Maddie. Ricky's under a lot of scrutiny right now. If you go nosing around, you may end up causing him more harm than help."

I bit my lip. I hated to admit it, but he did have a point. I had a bad feeling that while Ricky was no killer, he almost certainly was guilty of stepping out on Dana. A story the press would be dying to run with. The last thing I wanted to do was uncover undeniable evidence for them of Ricky and Irina doing the horizontal mambo (in addition to the vertical one).

I took a deep breath. "Okay, you're right."

Ramirez froze. Then he slowly raised one eyebrow at me. "Can I get that in writing? Preferably on a plaque that I can mount above our bed. 'My husband is right,'" he quoted.

I punched his shoulder. "Very funny, big guy."

He grinned, taking my hand. "You just enjoy the little ones while they're little and leave the murders to me. Trust me, Ricky will be fine."

I nodded. Hoping like heck he was right as he pulled me in for another deliciously beer-flavored kiss.

"Speaking of little ones... are they both asleep?" he murmured onto my lips.

I nodded. "Uh-huh."

A wicked gleam hit his eyes. "In that case, I've got six whole hours before I have to be back at the station," he said, his voice low and husky. "Let's make good use of them."

CHAPTER FIVE

———

"It was horrible, Maddie. I've never yelled so much in my life," Dana said, her voice hoarse in a way that spoke to the truth of her statement.

"So, The Fight continued at home, huh?" I asked, handing her a cup of coffee in my kitchen the next morning.

She nodded, her eyes red and puffy. She looked like she'd gotten even less sleep than I had and needed even more concealer. "All night."

"What did Ricky say?"

"That there was nothing going on between him and Irina. That he had no idea why she was in his dressing room." She paused. "Naked." Her face puckered as if in pain as she said the word.

"But you don't believe him."

Her lower lip quivered, adding to her pained look. "No! I mean, it would be one thing if he could give me a reason why she might be there. Any reason! But all he said was 'I dunno.'"

I had to admit, it wasn't the most convincing argument.

Dana slowly shook her head. "It was like he was incapable of giving me a straight answer."

"I'm so sorry," I said meaning it.

She nodded, sipping at her coffee. "Thanks." She paused. "Did you see the *Informer* this morning?"

I shook my head. "Bad?"

"Horrible. Allie called Ricky 'Dancing Death.'"

"Ouch," I agreed.

"The entire world thinks he's a killer now, Maddie." She buried her head in her arms on my kitchen counter. "Am I being naive?" she mumbled. "Am I being that blind blonde on *CSI* who can't see past her boyfriend's good looks to the cheating killer he is?"

I shook my head. "No. Honestly, I can't see Ricky hurting anyone either." I didn't speak to the cheating part. Truth was, he was looking guiltier on that score by the minute.

Dana lifted her head and took a deep breath. "I don't know what to do, Mads."

"Get him a lawyer."

"Oh, he has a lawyer," she informed me. "He called one last night when he got tired of fighting."

"And?"

"And there's nothing he can do. Unless Ricky is formally charged with something, the lawyer is useless. They're still going to crucify him in the media, and there's nothing anyone can do." She paused again, turning her big, blue eyes my way. "Until he's proven innocent."

"Why are you looking at me like that?" I asked, a bad feeling brewing in my stomach that had nothing to do with the strong coffee on an empty stomach.

"Come on, Maddie. He needs our help."

"*Our* help?"

"We're all he has, Maddie. No one else believes he's innocent. Honestly, I don't even think his lawyer believes him."

"I don't know. I mean, maybe we should leave this one to the authorities…" I trailed off, repeating Ramirez's warning from the night before.

"Please!" Dana clasped her hands in front of her face in a pleading motion. "We're Ricky's only hope. We have to find the real truth."

The real truth was exactly what I was afraid of.

"Ramirez promised me he'd find Irina's real killer and clear Ricky," I told her.

"So the cops have other suspects?" she asked, a glimmer of hope in her eyes.

I paused, coffee cup halfway to my lips. "Not exactly."

She collapsed her head back onto my counter. "I knew it. He's doomed."

I bit my lip. I hated that as much as I had faith in Ramirez, I was worried she may be right. Ramirez was not a one man show. If evidence started pointing Ricky's way, I knew that no matter how Ramirez might personally feel about our friend, it wasn't enough to convince the entire LAPD to keep him out of jail. Which, as much as I hated the idea of Ricky's cheating coming out in the press, was a way worse alternative.

I took a deep breath.

"Okay."

She lifted her head. "Okay?"

"Okay, we'll help Ricky."

She did a high-pitched squeal that might have spoken to dolphins and hugged me.

"But," I said, holding up a hand. "This is strictly an undercover operation. Meaning, we're just asking a few questions, and no one can know we're investigating."

While I hadn't actually technically promised Ramirez I'd stay away from the case, I had a bad feeling that beer-flavored kisses would be a thing of the past if he found out I rescinded my "you're right" plaque in favor of conducting a little investigation of my own.

Dana did a cross-her-heart thing. "Totally in the vault," she promised.

"Okay, then just let me make one phone call first," I said, grabbing my cell and hitting number three on my speed dial.

* * *

"Ohmigod, Mads, I was so super excited when you called me!" Marco squealed on my front porch half an hour later.

Marco was a part-time party planner to the stars and part-time receptionist at my stepfather's salon in Beverly Hills. He was slim, Hispanic, and gayer than a 1940's musical. One dash Marc Anthony and one dash JLo, Marco marched to the beat of his own fabulous drummer. Who mostly played Lady Gaga songs. Today he was dressed in a hot-pink leopard print top that looked painted onto his slim frame and a pair of black, leather pants that ended just below his calves. On his feet were pink espadrilles, and he'd tinted the ends of his spiky black hair hot pink to match.

"I'm so glad you were free today," I told him.

"For you? Of course," he said, air kissing me and flouncing into my living room. "So, tell me, where do we start investigating?"

I cleared my throat. "Uh, actually *you* start here."

Marco blinked heavily lined lashes at me. "What do you mean, doll-face?"

"I, uh, I actually called you here to babysit the twins so that Dana and I could go do some questioning."

Marco's face fell faster than the Dow Jones. "Noooooooo! But I wanna come tooooooo!"

"Please, Marco," I pleaded over his high-pitched whine, clasping my hands in front of myself. "They've already been fed, burped, changed and powdered. All you have to do is sit here and watch them play. And chances are they'll nap soon!"

Marco pouted, looking at the babies in question, lying on their backs on their play mat, both enamored with the tiny jungle animals dangling just above their reach.

"Pretty please," Dana chimed in. "I mean, we can't very well intimidate suspects with two babies in tow."

I frowned. *Intimidate* wasn't exactly on my to-do list. I was thinking more along the lines of polite questions of possible witnesses. But Dana was right about us going sans droolers. On the off chances that one of the people we talked to really was the one who had killed Irina, the last thing I wanted to do was expose my babies to a murderer.

"You know how much the babies love their Auntie Marco," I said, appealing to his maternal side.

Which seemed to soften him some, the pout turning into a nose-scrunch instead.

"It would mean so much to me," Dana said. Then added, "And to Ricky."

That did it. While every teen girl in the country had posters of Ricky on their walls, sixty percent of all gay men did as well. Including Marco.

"Would it mean enough for an autographed eight-by-ten?" he asked.

"Absolutely!" she promised.

"Fiiiine," Marco said, letting the word out on a sigh. "I'll watch Max and Livvie. Just don't be long. You know I don't do diapers," he added, scrunching his nose up again at the very thought of human feces.

"You are a prince," I said, giving him a quick kiss on the cheek and grabbing my purse before he could change his mind.

"And I want a full report when you come back!" he shouted over his shoulder as Dana and I made for the door.

"Fuller than a Texas beauty queen's bouffant," I promised. Then I hightailed it to my minivan before the bottle I'd just fed Livvie made it's way out the back end and toward Auntie Marco's delicate nose.

* * *

As any good crime drama addict knows, the first suspects on anyone's list are those closest to the victim. Ignoring the fact that she was found naked in Ricky's dressing room (which both Dana and I were doing with such fabulous denial that we should be in the running for Oscars), the next closest people to Irina were the ones she was with every day – her co-stars on *Dancing with Celebrities*. While ten celebrity and professional dancer pairs were part of the cast, only two others had been on the set the day Irina had died. Kaylie, the Teen Mom, and her partner, Sven, and Shaniqua, the tranny ex-football player and her partner, Joc. While I had a hard time seeing either star whacking Irina over the head to win DWC, it was at least a place to start.

Unfortunately, losing their star had temporarily shut down the DWC set. Meaning we had to find our suspects elsewhere.

Shaniqua, as it turned out, kept a surprisingly low social media profile. There was little info we could glean about her through our trusty friend Google. The expected news reports, pictures of her in drag, and about a dozen photos of her in the sequined number she'd danced the mambo in last week. No info about where she lived or how to contact her.

Luckily, the same couldn't be said for her co-star, Kaylie. She regularly tweeted photos of her place in Toluca Lake, and with a little more googling, Dana and I found an address posted on a virtual celebrities homes tour. I plugged it into my GPS, and twenty minutes later we were parked in front of a three-story McMansion flanked by palm trees, brick pavers, and a pair of large, stone gargoyles.

I looked to my left. Her neighbor had an RV parked in the drive of his modest, fifties-style ranch house. To the right was a tract home with a mid-sized sedan parked in the drive. Clearly one of these houses was not like the others.

Dana and I got out and followed the brick pathway along a circular drive to an ornate front door that looked more like it belonged on the entrance to a dungeon than a So. Cal residence.

I leaned on the doorbell, listening to it echo inside. A moment later the door was opened by a guy in a pair of neon yellow swim trunks and nothing else. He held a bong in one hand and a pink, plastic margarita glass in the shape of a cactus in the other.

"S'up," he said. Though I wasn't sure if it was a greeting or a question.

"Uh, hi. We're looking for Kaylie?" I asked.

"You the pizza guy?" he asked, squinting at me through half-baked eyes.

I put my hand on my hips. "Do I look like a pizza guy?" I countered. Personally, I thought the black stretch pants and red baby-doll top I'd paired with my favorite black wedges was a pretty stylish outfit. Granted, the pants were a size or two larger than my normal clothes, but they were certainly a cut above a Dominos uniform.

But the guy just shrugged. "Bummer. Kaylie's by the pool." He gestured vaguely somewhere behind him, which I took as an invitation to enter.

Dana followed me into a foyer featuring pink marble tiles, a huge chandelier dripping with pink crystals, and walls covered in velvet flocked wallpaper in hues of… you guessed it… pink. The entire effect had the feel of walking into a life-sized Disney princess dollhouse.

Down a hallway just ahead of us I spotted a pair of French doors leading out to the backyard. I led Dana through, leaving Kaylie's greeter to wait for his pizza as we stepped outside onto a large patio. At the edge was a swimming pool filled with inflatable floaties. A brunette in a bikini occupied one while two more guys in swim trunks splashed each other in the deep end of the pool. Sitting near the steps, wearing a hot pink bikini and sipping from another cactus shaped glass, sat Kaylie. She had platinum hair, accented with pink streaks, dark eyes rimmed in even darker eyeliner, and hot pink lipstick on her lips that I noticed were just a shade plumper than last season. As were her boobs. Apparently consenting to have her questionable parenting skills televised had paid off.

Sitting beside her in the shallow end was her golden ticket – her two-year-old son Brady. He was wearing a pair of Spiderman water wings and blowing bubbles in the water.

"Kaylie?" I asked as we approached.

She looked up, shading her eyes with one manicured hand as she squinted my way.

"You the new nanny?" she asked.

That's it. I was totally going shopping for a new outfit tomorrow.

"No. We're friends of Ricky's," Dana said.

Kaylie's gaze shifted to Dana. "Oh. Right. 'Sup, bitches."

I was about to take offense, when I realized by the expectant look on her face that it was just her version of a friendly greeting.

"Uh, s'up," I responded back.

"You're, like, Ricky's GF or something, right?" Kaylie said, addressing Dana.

"GF?" I asked.

"Girlfriend," Dana supplied, apparently more well-versed in Teen Speak than I was. "And, yeah, I am."

"Bummer. Sorry," Kaylie told her. "What a TCA, right?"

"TCA?" I looked to Dana to translate.

"Total Cheating Asshole," Dana said, her face scrunching up, eyes tearing.

"Ah. Anyway," I said, quickly changing the subject, "we were wondering if we could ask you a couple of questions about Irina."

"Oh, yeah. Totally sad about that." Kaylie pursed her lips and nodded. "I hear production is going to be shut down for, like, the whole week."

"Did you know Irina well?" I asked.

Kaylie shrugged. "Not really. She kinda kept to herself. Ricky was really the only person she talked to, you know?" She paused, then turned to Dana. "Sorry."

Dana did the scrunched face thing again.

"What about the other dancers," I asked. "Was she close with any of them?"

Kaylie shook her head, hair falling in front of her eyes like a highlighted sheepdog. "Not that I noticed. I mean, we hardly ever saw the other contestants." She paused, turning to me. "We all rehearsed on set on different days. Shaniqua, me and Ricky were all on the same day, but the rest of the cast was split up on other days," she explained.

"And she didn't seem particularly close to anyone from your day?" I asked.

She shook her head. "Irina was Russian, and Sven and Joc are both from Norway. The language barrier was, like, way hard. I don't think she really hung out with anyone else. You know, except for Ricky."

"What about-" I started.

But I didn't get to finish as Dana blurted out, "Was Ricky cheating on me?"

I cringed, not wanting to hear the answer to that.

But Kaylie just shrugged again. "I dunno. I mean, it wasn't like they made out on set or anything."

I did an internal sigh of relief.

Dana did an audible one.

"But I did see her going into his dressing room last week."

Dana sucked in a breath beside me. "You did?" she squeaked out, eyes pooling again.

"Uh-huh. She was totally cagey about it, too. Like, looking over her shoulder to see if anyone was watching and stuff."

"Was Ricky with her?" Dana asked.

"No. I figured he was inside waiting for her or something."

"Ohmigod…" Dana trailed off in a high-pitched squeak.

"Back to yesterday," I quickly said, trying to re-direct the conversation again. "Did you notice anything odd on the set? Or anything out of the ordinary with Irina?"

Kaylie shrugged again. I was beginning to think it was her signature move. "What's out of the ordinary? Irina was, like, such a W-O."

I turned to Dana for an interpretation.

"Weird-o," she supplied, getting her sniffles under control.

"Weird how?" I asked Kaylie.

"She was, like, all loud and screamy and stuff. She was so not friendly. I mean, ask Shaniqua."

"Why? Did something happen between her and Shaniqua?" I asked, jumping on the statement.

Kaylie nodded vigorously, her hair covering her eyes again. "Uh, yeah! She totally laid into Shaniqua the other day."

"They argued?" I asked.

She nodded. "Dude, it was like World War three. I caught them backstage after Irina's number in that black, off the shoulder dress."

"The mambo," I supplied, having DVR-ed the episode myself.

"Right. Anyway, Shaniqua was like totally yelling at Irina."

"What was she saying?" I asked.

Kaylie shrugged. "I dunno. I didn't really pay attention. It was like something about her being a liar."

"What did she lie about?"

"Sorry. You'd have to ask Shaniqua."

Trust me, I intended to.

"Is that a margarita?" Dana asked, gesturing to Kaylie's glass.

"Uh, yeah," the teen answered.

"I could so use a drink right now," Dana hinted.

Kaylie handed her the glass. "Knock yourself out.

"Aren't you a bit young to be drinking?" I asked, watching my friend knock back the entire contents of the glass.

Kaylie did her signature shrug again. "If I'm old enough to shoot a person out of my hooha, I think I deserve a drink."

I had to admit, I couldn't argue with her there.

We thanked Kaylie for her time and left just as the pizza guy was arriving. (Who, by the way, was dressed nothing like me.)

Dana agreed with me that talking to Shaniqua was our next move. Unfortunately, we had no idea where to find the former athlete. Fortunately, I knew of one person who would.

I slipped on my hands-free earpiece and dialed as I pulled back into traffic.

Two rings in, it was answered by a female voice.

"Bender," she barked as a greeting.

Tina Bender was the gossip columnist at the *L.A. Informer* and knew everything about everyone who was anyone in Hollywood. And, as much as I hated going to the press for help, Tina and I shared one very important common bond - a mutual distrust of Allie Quick. Tina was everything that Allie was not: brunette, tom-boyish, funky, and outspoken to a fault. Tina had purple hair, drove a motorcycle, and dated a bodyguard with muscles the size of basketballs. When I'd first met her, I'll admit, I'd been a little intimidated. But, after getting to know her a little, I'd realized that not only was Tina softer on the inside than she appeared on the outside, but she was also the most highly connected person in Hollywood. A trait that made her my first choice for tracking down Shaniqua.

"Hey, Tina. It's Maddie Springer. Listen, I was wondering if you could do me a small favor?"

"Depends," Tina said, and I got the distinct impression she was chewing something. "What kind of favor?"

"I'm trying to track down the address of a celebrity, and I was wondering if you might be able to help."

"It's possible," Tina said, definitely chewing this time, then doing a swallowing sound. "Who is the celeb?"

"Shaniqua Jones."

There was a pause on Tina's end. Then finally she asked, "This wouldn't have anything to do with the murder on the set of DWC that Allie's working on, would it?"

I squinted one eye shut, cringing just a little. "Yes?" I said, though it came out more of a question.

"Sweet. I'm in," Tina responded. "Just promise that you come to me first with the story, not Barbie. Cool?"

I said a silent thank-you to the gods of mutual distrust as I agreed, and Tina promised to make a few calls and get back to me.

Dana and I pulled into a Starbucks to wait, though Dana said she was too upset to eat anything. I, on the other hand, was starving. I grabbed a chicken salad from their refrigerated section, ate the entire thing, then contemplated the bakery case. My willpower and I were just having a heated argument over a maple scone when my cell buzzed to life in my purse. I slipped it out, expecting news from Tina. What I saw instead was a text from my mom.

sale at macys. i have coupons. u in?

I raised an eyebrow. Macy's was a good few steps up from her last shopping excursion. And I *did* have some time to kill while waiting for Tina's info. And I *was* without twins for the next couple of hours. And my wardrobe *had* just been mistaken for that of a pizza guy.

"Dana, mind a trip to the mall?" I asked my still-sulking companion.

Her eyes welled up. "Ricky and I used to go to the mall together all the time. We're never going to the mall together again, are we? Our days of together things are over!"

Oh brother.

I texted my mom back: *yes, in desperate need of retail therapy. b there in 20*

Unfortunately, there was a wreck on the 101, and it took another forty minutes before we were making our way through the Beverly Center to Macy's. Mom was already hard at work in the clearance racks, sniffing out a deal like a bloodhound. Beside her was her best friend, Mrs. Rosenblatt, arms loaded with dresses in colors bright enough to require sunglasses. Mrs.

Rosenblatt weighed three-hundred-plus pounds, had gone through five husbands, and worked on the Venice Boardwalk on weekends as a psychic medium. Anywhere else, she would have been considered an odd duck. In L.A. she blended right in.

"Maddie!" Mom called, giving me a cheerful wave from behind a rack of 50% off blazers in bright fuchsia. "I saved a couple of sweaters for you. I think they're perfect for this cool, winter weather."

"What cool weather? It's seventy-nine and sunny."

She ignored me, shoving the garments my way.

I held up the first one. It was yellow with a Dalmatian's face embroidered on the front.

"I'm not really a big dog person, Mom," I said, trying to be kind.

She shook her head. "But it's 75% off."

"Gee, I wonder why?" Dana mumbled.

"Try the other one on," Mom instructed, ignoring her too.

I held Number Two up to my torso. It featured orange and black horizontal stripes. "I'm not sure this is exactly flattering," I hedged.

"Nonsense, you look lovely in anything," my mom said.

"Um, thanks?"

"Besides," Mrs. Rosenblatt jumped in, "you're all ready for next Halloween."

I gently put the sweater back on the clearance table behind her. "I think we'll go check out the petites section," I told her, escaping before she could force a sweater on Dana, too.

While Dana was far from petite, she tagged along, saying she wasn't really in the mood to buy anything today anyway. I understood, but it was a rare moment out for me without babies. I was going to take advantage of it. (Especially since I had a 15% off coupon from my mom plus an extra 10% off if I used my Macy's card. I was no math whiz, but that equaled a good deal.)

Two tops, one pair of jeans, and a fabulous pair of boots later my Macy's card had gotten a good workout, and my cell finally buzzed in my purse with Tina's name in the readout.

I looked down at the text and just barely restrained myself from doing a happy dance right there in the perfume section.

Shaniqua Jones at the Firefly Gym. 215 Honeywell Street, West Hollywood. Go scoop Allie.

CHAPTER SIX

———

An hour later we were parked in front of the Firefly Gym in West Hollywood.

Where Hollywood was known for its glamorous stars, footprints in cement, and tourist attractions galore, West Hollywood had a much different vibe. One that was colored in rainbows and sang along to Judy Garland records. The West Hollywood male population outnumbered women five to one and adhered to the strict rules of no white after Labor Day, no loafers with socks, and no closed closet doors. Personally, I thought it was the single most fashion-forward city in the world. At least as far as menswear was concerned.

The Firefly Gym was located at Hancock and Santa Monica, across the street from an organic smoothie shop and a salon featuring a special on their gentleman's "Man-i-Cure". Dana and I pushed inside the doors and immediately stuck out like sore, female thumbs.

The walls were painted a vibrant hot pink, men in spandex lined the walls doing curls, pull-ups and lunges, and an ABBA tune was being pumped in through hidden speakers. I had a feeling that we had just entered a meat market to rival any on Food Network. And we were distinctly not on the menu.

"May I help you?" asked a slim, African American man sitting behind the front desk. He wore an outfit straight out of Jane Fonda's first work-out video, complete with turquoise leg warmers and matching headband.

"Uh, we're looking for Shaniqua Jones?" I asked. "We were told she was here?"

The guy nodded. "Sure. She's with her trainer. Just a minute, honey," he said, then picked up a phone receiver from the desk in the shape of a pair of lips. "Shani has visitors at the front desk," he said. Then he addressed us. "She'll be right out."

Dana and I thanked him, then took a seat on two of the yellow plastic chairs lining the reception area. Another ABBA song later, Shaniqua emerged, making her way from the back of the gym.

Shaniqua had exactly the type of physique you'd expect when you heard the word "linebacker." She was tall, broad, and meaty. Thick shoulders, a thick neck, and wide set eyes that were sunken back from her forehead. It was a look that had intimidated many a man on the gridiron, but, unfortunately, made for one of the ugliest women I'd ever seen. While she'd done her best with thick eyeliner and contouring bronzer, her features were still distinctly male, and there weren't enough Spanx in the world to help her achieve an hour-glass shape. Today she was wearing a spandex leotard in lemon yellow, matched with a pair of black yoga pants and lemon yellow sneakers. Her forehead was shiny with perspiration,and her blonde wig was slightly askew, speaking to the difficulty of the personal training session we'd interrupted.

As Shaniqua made her way into reception, the headband-wearing guy nodded in our direction. Shaniqua's eyes shifted our way, and I could feel her mentally sizing us up like she had her opponents on the field.

"Uh, hi," I said, waving. "We haven't formally met, but I saw you on the DWC set yesterday. I'm Maddie," I said, extending my hand.

She took it, shaking it in a grip that was nearly crushing.

"Dana," my best friend added, doing a repeat of my shake.

Shaniqua nodded. "Yeah. I recognize you. Ricky's girl, right?" she asked. Her voice was deep, making no effort to conceal the gender it had been born into, and had an East Coast tinge to it. Not surprising since he'd spent several years playing for one of the NFC East's best teams.

"Right," Dana agreed. "We were wondering if we could ask you a couple of questions?"

"About?" Shaniqua asked, raising one artfully drawn eyebrow.

"Irina," I jumped in.

She shot me a look that said she was trying hard to muster up the socially acceptable level of sympathy. "A crying shame what happened to her."

"You were close?" I asked, noting the distinct lack of crying.

"Well, I wouldn't say close, but we were colleagues of a sort, now, weren't we?"

"Did you get along?"

He grinned. "It would be stupid of us not to. The press would eat that sort of story up."

Hmm. I couldn't help but notice she was expertly not answering any of my questions.

"They're currently busy eating up a story of Ricky being called a killer," Dana pointed out.

"Yeah, that really sucks. I feel for the guy, you know? The press can be brutal." The suddenly soft look in his eyes told me he had first-hand knowledge of that fact.

"Did you happen to see anything the day Irina died?" I asked.

"What sort of anything?"

I wished I knew. "Anyone on the set who didn't belong there? Anything odd or suspicious? Anyone going into Ricky's dressing room?"

"Other than Ricky," Dana clarified.

But Shaniqua shook her head, the wig falling another inch to the right. "No. Sorry. I was rehearsing in the dance studio while they set the lighting and music for Ricky and Irina's number.

"Did you see Irina at all that day?"

She nodded. "I passed her in the hall a few times."

"Did you talk to her?"

She shrugged. "I guess. But just chit-chatty stuff. What color dress was she wearing, what song was she using. Normal stuff, you know?"

"So, you didn't argue with her?" I asked, slowly, watching her reaction.

"No. Why would I?"

"We heard that you had a disagreement with her last week," Dana supplied.

Shaniqua crossed her arms over her broad chest, her eyes guarded as they shifted from Dana to me. "Where did you hear that?"

I shrugged. "Around," I said, non-committally. Not that I felt any particular loyalty to Kaylie, but if Shaniqua had anything to do with Irina's death, the last thing I wanted to do was provide her a motive for a second one.

"Damned press," Shaniqua mumbled under her breath. "See, I knew there was a leak on the set. Who is it, huh? Grip? PA? That damned lighting guy?"

I bit my lip. By the way the news of Irina's death had hit the *Informer* website at lightening speed, I was pretty sure there was a press leak, too. However, since this particular tidbit hadn't actually come to me from that leak I redirected her back to the original question. "So it's true? You and Irina did fight?"

"Yeah, so what? We argued. Big deal."

"About what?" Dana asked.

Shaniqua shifted her attention to Dana. "She was cheating."

I felt Dana tense beside me.

Uh-oh. I almost hated to ask…

"Cheating?"

"With the votes."

I paused. That wasn't the kind of cheating I'd been bracing against. "You mean, the votes to stay on the show?"

She nodded. "Yeah. She was totally stacking them in her favor."

"Wait, how was she doing that?" I asked. As a weekly voter myself, I was familiar with the way the voting went. At the end of the show, the host flashed phone numbers for each pair of dancers. Fans could either call in or text for their favorite. Whoever had the most calls was safe, and the pair with the least went home on the following night's live elimination show. It seemed pretty straightforward, and I didn't quite see how one could cheat the system.

"Irina was buying votes," Shaniqua told me.

"From whom?"

"The Russians, for one. But who knows, maybe several countries."

"And how do you know this?"

"I overhead her talking to a guy in her dressing room last week. Most of it was in Russian. But then I caught part of it in English. She said that the show didn't air in Russia, so no one would know. Then the guy said something back in Russian, and she told him that with those votes, she could guarantee that she'd win."

"Then what happened?" I asked.

"Then I got called to set, so I didn't hear anything else. But I think it was pretty straight-forward what was going on. She was buying Russian votes from this guy. I mean, the producers don't care where you call from to vote. They just care that it's between the two hours after the show ends. She could have had the whole of Europe calling in for all I know."

I pursed my lips. While it sounded like Shaniqua was making a few leaping conclusions with the partial conversation she'd heard, they didn't seem all that far-fetched.

"Did you confront Irina about the conversation?" Dana asked her.

She nodded. "You bet I did! Hey, I've spent my whole life playing fair. I wasn't going to lose now because some Euro-trash tart was stacking the deck. I called her out. Said she was going to play fair, or I was going to report her to the producers."

"And what was her response?" I asked.

"She said if I knew what was good for me I'd keep my mouth shut." Shaniqua laughed. "Can you imagine that? This little five-foot-nothing thing threatening *me*?"

I had to admit, that would take some *cojones*. I was feeling a little intimidated just standing next to Shaniqua's hulking frame, never mind being on her bad side.

"Anyway, I told her she better not try it. That I was on to her and her voting scheme, and I would tell all."

"And did you?"

She shook her head. "Never had the chance. We didn't get to dance this week, so I had nothing for the producers to investigate yet. She got off lucky," she said, the threat still hanging in her voice.

I wasn't all that sure that being bludgeoned to death in the buff was what I'd call "lucky." And while I was inclined to believe Shaniqua about that being the end of her altercation with Irina, if there was one thing I knew about Shaniqua it was that she knew how to play a role. She'd played the macho jock her whole life as Shawn. So was she telling the truth now or was she playing the role of the innocent bystander when really she'd killed to keep the playing field fair?

"The Russian guy with Irina. What can you tell me about him?" I asked, shifting focus.

Shaniqua shrugged. "Not much. I didn't actually see the guy. I just overheard the conversation."

"Any idea who he was? Or how Irina knew him?" I grasped.

But she shook her head. "Sorry. Trust me, if I knew who the guy was, I'd pay him a little visit myself. Give that cheating bastard a piece of my mind," she said, clenching her fists.

I gulped, hoping I was never in a position to receive any part of her mind. I thanked Shaniqua for her time, then Dana and I made our way back out to the parking lot.

"So, you think she was telling the truth about Irina buying votes?" Dana asked hopefully as we walked back to my car.

I nodded. "I can't see why she would lie about it now."

"You think maybe it had something to do with her death?"

"I think," I cautiously answered, "that we should talk to that Russian guy."

Dana nodded. "Agreed."

Then I looked down at the time on my cell phone readout. "But it may have to wait until tomorrow. It's almost six."

She gave me a blank look.

"Ramirez will be home soon."

"And..."

"And, if he finds out I've been looking into Irina's death on my own, he'll kill me."

"That's never stopped you before."

She had a point. "I know, but things are different now."
Dana scrunched up her nose. "The babies?"

"According to my husband, I'm supposed to let him solve murders while I sit home wiping butts and watching *Dora the Explorer*," I told her.

"I thought you liked Dora?"

"That's beside the point," I said, waving her off. "The point is, I'm still just as capable of solving this crime as I was before my uterus fulfilled its purpose."

"Only, you're going to have to do it by sneaking around behind Ramirez's back."

I nodded. "Exactly."

Dana shook her head at me. "I don't get you married people."

"Trust me. There comes a point in a marriage where the best thing you can do to keep the peace is keep your mouth shut. Now come on. I gotta get home, pronto."

With traffic, it was almost forty-minutes before we finally pulled up in front of my bungalow. And even before I exited the car, I heard the sound of baby lullabies blasting at top volume from the interior of my house.

Uh-oh.

I made a bee-line for the front door, pulling it open and covering my ears against the assaulting strains of "Hush Little Baby" being sung over the speaker system. Marco was sitting cross-legged on the floor with a pair of socks held onto his ears by a sparkly pink headband. Mine, I noticed.

"What is going on?" I yelled.

"What?"

"What is going on!?"

"I can't hear you," Marco yelled back.

"What-" I shook my head, giving up, and crossed to the iPod dock in the corner, hitting the pause button. Silence immediately descended.

I took a deep breath, my ears ringing. "What was that about?" I asked.

Marco shrugged, taking the socks off of his ears. "It was the only way I could get them to stop crying. I had to drown them out."

I was about to tell him that drowning out a baby's cries was not in Babysitting 101, when I noticed both of my babies sitting in their swings, gurgling happily. Huh. What do you know, it looked like he was right. They did like the loud music.

I crossed the room and looked more closely at my kids. They were both dressed in pink.

"Um, why is my son wearing a pink dress?" I asked, turning again to the babysitting wonder.

"I had to change them," Marco said. Then he gave me a dirty look. "They pooed, Maddie. And it was eeeeeeverywhere," he said, drawing out the word as he gestured around the room.

"And?"

"And, once I finally got them clean and put diapers on, I kind of lost track of which was which. And *no way* was I taking those diapers off again. So I put them both in a gender neutral color."

I was about to point out that pink wasn't exactly the most gender neutral color when I looked down at Marco's hot pink ensemble and realized that rationale would be lost on him.

"Well, thanks for watching them," I said instead. Okay, so he hadn't followed the *What to Expect the First Year*'s rules on baby care, but both babies looked clean and happy. I couldn't argue with that.

"You're welcome," Marco said, tossing the socks and headband onto my coffee table. "But next time, I'm coming with you."

I nodded in agreement, picking up the closest pink bundle and doing a diaper check. Female. I put her back in her seat and grabbed her pink-clad brother from beside her, then headed for the changing table before my husband got home and saw his son in sparkly, pink tulle.

CHAPTER SEVEN

―――――

Ramirez snuck out of bed somewhere between the twins' pre-dawn feeding and their synchronized morning battle cry, around 7am. Which normally would have left me feeling exhausted and abandoned but today fit in perfectly with my plans. At least I didn't have to lie to my husband about where I was going.

I showered, dressed, grabbed my diet breakfast bar and even had time to put on a little mascara between Livvie's and Max's crying jags by the time Dana showed up on my doorstep an hour later.

She looked as if she'd slept about as little as I had. Her hair was thrown into a messy chic bun that was far more messy than chic, her eyes were red and rimmed in dark circles, and her usual glam self was shoved into a pair of capri style sweats, a tank top with black bra straps showing beneath, and a pair of yellow Crocs on her feet.

I gasped. "Dana, what on earth are you wearing?"

She looked down at her feet. "What?"

"Those!"

"What? They're Crocs."

"Yes they are," I said, nodding vigorously. "And are you a toddler going to a play date at the park?"

She cocked her head at me. "Um, no."

"Then what are you doing wearing them?!" I paused, coming up with a better question. "Why do you even *own* them?"

She sighed. "What does it matter? Who cares how I look? My life is over anyway," she said, flopping onto my sofa. "Ricky didn't come home last night."

"Oh, honey." I grabbed her in a hug, ignoring the funky scent telling me she'd skipped the shower this morning, too.

"He texted," she told me. "Said he was staying at his Malibu house hiding out from the press."

I nodded. "I can understand that."

"But I think he was really hiding out from me." Her voice cracked on the last word.

I shook my head violently from side to side. "No. I'm sure that's not true."

Dana sniffed, wiping her nose with the back of her hand. "I don't know what to do, Maddie. I miss him. But I don't want to miss him. I shouldn't miss him. He cheated on me. At least, I think he cheated on me. I'm pretty sure he cheated on me."

"I think," I said, handing her a tissue, "that Ricky will have a perfectly good explanation for everything."

She shot me a look.

"Okay, fine. That was a lie. I was trying to be comforting."

She sniffed again. "Thanks. I appreciate it. But you know what would be more comforting?" she asked.

"What?"

"Ice cream."

I froze. Dana craving ice cream was like me craving wheat grass – a sign that something was seriously wrong. "You mean like, soy frozen yogurt, right?" I clarified.

Dana went into my kitchen and opened the freezer inspecting the contents. "Actually, where do you keep your Haagen-Dazs?" she asked.

"I don't have any Haagen-Dazs. I'm on a diet."

Dana grabbed a Weight Watchers fat-free, dairy-free, low-carb popsicle. She scrunched up her nose. "I think we're gonna need a Dairy Queen run."

"Who are you, and what have you done with my best friend?"

She ignored me, digging into the deep recesses of my freezer for any pre-diet items I might have forgotten. Best of luck to her. I'd already beaten her to anything even remotely resembling chocolate or sugar.

I poured myself a cup of coffee in a to-go mug and texted Mom.

free 2 watch twins 2day?

Two minutes later her response came through. *of course!! got pressies 4 them on sale yesterday. brt*

While I was relieved to have a babysitter, I was a little nervous at the "pressies". As much as I refused to fall fashion victim to my mom's coupon craze, I was determined not to let her stunt my babies' fashion growth either.

Twenty minutes later my fear was realized as Mom showed up on my doorstep with a brown paper shopping bag. "Lookie what Grandma has..." she sing-songed to my diapered duo. Then she pulled out a yellow sweater with a huge orange duck embroidered across the front.

"Oh... that's..." I trailed off as she pulled out matching yellow pants. Complete with webbed duck feet. And a yellow hat with a knitted beak attached.

"What do you think, Mads?" she asked.

"I think it's time for me to go." Hey, that was the kindest response I could come up with.

"Isn't it adorable?" Mom asked.

"It's... something."

But Mom didn't take the hint, pulling out another matching outfit in yellow. "I got one for each of them. They can be little duckie twins!"

"Don't you think the webbed feet might be a bit, um, uncomfortable?" I asked, doing my best to save my children.

"Nonsense. They're adorable," Mom said, grabbing the nearest baby, pulling off his blue onesie, and duckifying him.

I swear he gave me a pitiful "save me" look as she stuck the duck-beak hat on him.

I leaned down and kissed Max's cheek. "Sorry, buddy. I tried," I whispered, feeling twice as guilty now for leaving him. I did a repeat with Livvie, promising her that I'd take her to Bloomingdales this weekend and make it up to her.

Once we left my kids to fend for themselves against the duck transformation, our first stop on our quest to find Irina's mysterious Russian visitor (after Dairy Queen, of course) was at the UBN studios.

As we well knew, everyone who entered the network studios set had to check in with the guards up front. Which meant so had our mystery man with the voting scheme.

We pulled up to the guardhouse at the front gates to the UBN complex, checking out the guards on duty. There were two: one monitoring cars coming in, the other monitoring those exiting the studios. The first guy was in his forties, wore a military buzz cut, and a pot belly that looked like he was due in about two months. His mouth was set in a tight line, his eyes hidden behind a pair of mirrored glasses, his uniform straining against his chest as he crossed his arms in front of him. The second guy was the complete opposite, looking like he was straight out of a Disney movie – big ears, big nose, and a big grin that he flashed at every leaving car. He waved to a couple in a Mercedes as they passed by. "Have a wonderful day!" he shouted after them, as Sergeant Buzz Cut approached our car.

"Name?" he asked, his eyes on the clipboard in his hands.

"Dana Dashel," Dana responded, leaning over the console to be heard from my passenger seat.

He paused a moment, scanning the page. Finally he found her name. "Go ahead," he motioned.

"Uh, actually, we were wondering if we could have moment of your time?" I asked, glancing in my rearview mirror to make sure we weren't holding up a line of impatient starlets.

Sergeant Buzz Cut looked up from his clipboard and gave me a long stare. "Why?"

"You keep track of who goes in and out, right?" I asked, gesturing to the gates.

"Of course. All visitors to the UBN studios must pass clearance," he said as if reciting a page from the UBN Security Guard Handbook.

"We're interested in someone who visited the studio last week. We were wondering if maybe you could give us his name?" I asked, flashing him my best "pretty please" smile.

But his lips stayed set into the same tight line. "All information regarding visitors to the UBN studios is at level one security."

I just barely resisted the urge to roll my eyes. The guy was protecting sitcom scripts, not government nukes.

"He was foreign?" Dana put in. "Russian possibly?"

"All information regarding visitors-" Buzz Cut started to repeat.

But his cartoon character counterpart on the other side of the guardhouse cut in, approaching us. "Russian, you said?" he asked.

I nodded vigorously.

"What day did he come in?" Cartoon asked, consulting his own clipboard.

Buzz Cut scowled at him, clearly wishing his colleague took security more seriously.

"We're not exactly sure. Last week," I said.

"But it would have been after Wednesday," Dana added, noting the last air date of DWC.

Cartoon's eyebrows furrowed, a frown settling between them in an exaggerated motion as he stared down at his board, scanning entries. "Let's see… Thursday… I'm not seeing any unfamiliar names…"

I mentally crossed my fingers as he flipped to the next page.

"Friday… nothing that stands out…"

"It's possible," I said, having a light bulb moment, "that he might have come in with Irina Sokolov."

Cartoon flipped back a page again. "Okay, yes. I have Irina and passenger on Friday afternoon."

"Just passenger?" I asked, feeling my heart sink.

Cartoon shrugged. "Sorry."

Buzz Cut grunted, his lips turning up into a small I-told-you-so smile.

"You didn't happen to see the passenger, did you?" Dana asked, leaning over my lap again.

"Sorry. That would have been my lunch break. Bill, here, was the only one on duty then." Cartoon gestured to his military friend.

We all turned to Buzz Cut.

His mouth turned down into that straight line again.

"Please?" I pleaded. "Surely it's not against any rules to describe what a visitor to the UBN studios just looks like?"

He paused a moment as if mentally reviewing the handbook.

We all held our breath in silence, waiting for his reply.

"Fine," he finally said. "Though I don't remember much about the guy."

"Anything you can remember is helpful," I assured him, leaning forward in my seat, too.

"Dark hair, pale complexion, average features."

He was right. That wasn't much help.

"Anything distinct about him at all?" Dana grasped. "A scar? A tattoo?"

The guy gave her a look. "What do you think this is, a Scorsese movie?"

She bit her lip.

"Look, he just looked like a normal guy," Buzz Cut told us.

"What was he wearing?" I grasped.

He took a deep breath, as if reaching into the recesses of his memory. "I didn't notice his clothes. But he was wearing a big diamond stud in his right ear. I noticed because my wife is always going on about how she wants a few more carats in her ring," he explained.

Well, it wasn't much to go on, but at least it was something.

As we'd worked on Sergeant Buzz Cut a line had begun to form behind us, so we thanked him for his time and did a U-turn, pulling back out of the studios on Cartoon's side and exiting to the tune of his, "Have a wonderful day!"

"So, now what?" Dana asked as we pulled away from the lot.

I shrugged. I'll admit, a dark-haired guy wearing an oversized earring wasn't a whole lot to go on.

"Maybe we should go to talk to Lana," I decided, "my friend in wardrobe." What with the murder, I never had gotten a chance to ask her about the alleged thefts on the set. I had no idea if one thing had anything to do with the other, but it was a bit of a coincidence both of them happening at the same time.

Dana nodded in the seat next to me. "Fine. But then let's get some lunch. I'm starving. I want pizza."

I glanced over at her. "Are you sure you're okay?" I asked.

She gave me a blank look. "What? A girl can't have a pizza craving every now and then?"

In the almost twenty years I had known Dana, I had never seen her have a pizza craving.

* * *

With the *Dancing with Celebrities* set still shut down, I took a chance that we might be able to find Lana at her boutique on Melrose. After circling a parking garage off Fairfax a dizzying number of times, we finally found a spot on the third level.

One elevator ride and three blocks of kitschy boutiques later, we spotted The Sunshine State, a bohemian shop whose windows were filled with imported saris, African inspired maxi skirts, and cute little white bodices with Eastern European flair.

As we approached, I watched the doors open and a woman emerge, tossing her platinum blonde Barbie hair over one shoulder as she tugged the hem of her mini skirt down over a pair of perfectly tanned thighs.

I felt my eyes narrow in recognition.

Allie Quick.

She must have felt my stare, as her gaze turned my way. It took her a moment for recognition to set in, but when it did, her eyes went round, her cherry red lips doing a mirror image in a perfect little "O".

"Ohmigod, Maddie! Is that yoooooou?" she asked, practically squealing the last part in dog whistle levels.

"Hi, Allie," I answered, as she attacked me with air kisses.

"Wow, it's been like forever, right?" she asked, her bimbo accent tinting her voice.

Here was the thing about Allie: she wasn't a bad kid. But she was a kid. She was like an exaggerated, twenty-five year old version of me - only cutesier, bubblier, and blonder.

Words like "whatevs", "deets" and "totes" flowed freely from her lips, her nails were long and embellished with rhinestones, and ninety-percent of her wardrobe was some shade of pink. Her skirts were short, her necklines low, and her boobs a very healthy D cup. She looked like the ultimate dumb blonde, an act she played to the fullest to work male informants all over L.A. She'd graduated top of her class from UCLA journalism school, a position that I had thought would land her a gig on the *Times* staff. Instead, for some reason she'd decided to write for the *L.A. Informer*. I had a feeling it had less to do with a love of gossip and more to do with her feelings toward the managing editor, Felix. A fact I wasn't quite sure how I felt about. There was a time when I would have thought Felix had feelings for me. Not that we'd ever indulged in those feelings (much), but I never quite got what Felix saw in her. (Beyond the D cups, that is.)

While Allie and I had crossed paths a handful of times, the years and managing editors between us had kept the term "friends" at a distance. It was more like we had a healthy tolerance for each other.

"How are you, Allie?" I asked.

"I'm totally great. Got this new story I'm working on. Very good stuff," she added, nodding and grinning in a knowing way.

"Hmm..." I mused. "That wouldn't happen to be the one where a dancer was killed on the set of *Dancing with Celebrities*, would it?"

Allie blinked, playing innocent. "Whatever would give you that idea?"

"You called my boyfriend 'Dancing Death,'" Dana said.

Allie beamed. "Cool alliteration, right?"

Dana narrowed her eyes.

"Speaking of Ricky," Allie said, completely ignoring the steam about to burst from Dana's ears. "How is he taking all of this? I assume he's maintaining his innocence? Rumor has it he's holed up in his Malibu estate. That true?"

I shook my head at her. "Uh-uh. No way. You're not getting a story out of us."

She shrugged. "Can't blame a girl for trying, right?"

That was debatable.

"What were you doing in Lana's store?" I asked, gesturing to the boutique behind her.

"Oh, you know. Just following up on a story."

"About the thefts on the DWC set?" I asked.

Allie paused. "Wow, you seem to know all about my stories already."

"Felix told me you were on it."

"He did, did he?" she asked, her face a blank.

"Coincidence that the thefts occurred just before Irina died?" I asked, feeling out what she might know.

But her freshly spray-tanned face remained a blank. "You know, it's been great seeing you again," she said, sidestepping the question as she looked down at her cell phone. "But I've gotta run. Felix is taking me to this new restaurant, Tapas Mexicana, tonight, so I can fill him in on all my *gory* details." She emphasized the word for my benefit. "So I'm off to get a fresh pedi. Wouldn't do to arrive looking shlumpy, would it? See you ladies later!" she called, holding her phone up as she practically skipped past us toward the parking garage we'd just come from.

"You don't think that shlumpy comment was directed at me, was it?" Dana asked, looking down at her sweats.

I was such a good friend that I didn't answer that question. "Come on, let's go see Lana," I said, instead, pushing through the boutique's front doors.

A girl with pink hair in tall spikes and three earrings in her nose stood behind the counter, folding colorful silk scarves. A blue one caught my eye, and I wondered if it would be wrong to do just a little shopping while we were there.

"Welcome to The Sunshine State," she said. "Anything in particular I can help you find today?"

"Actually, we were wondering if Lana was in?" I asked. "I'm a friend of hers from college," I explained.

The girl nodded, her hair, I noticed, not moving an inch. Impressive. "Sure. She's in the back. Let me just go see if she's free."

I thanked her and watched her disappear through a storeroom door, then snuck a glance at the price tag on the blue scarf. It was in the 'painful' range, though not totally into Top-

Ramen-for-a-month territory. I momentarily weighed the necessity of two college funds. I mean, wasn't one doctor in the family enough?

"Maddie, is that you?"

I turned and saw Lana standing in the storeroom doorway. She was wearing a long, flowing maxi-skirt, a skin-tight T-shirt, and a red version of the scarf I'd seen her assistant folding. To cap it off, she wore a pair of white clogs on her feet that were big, clunky, and looked to be carved from actual wood. Honestly? Not shoes I would ever be caught dead in, but somehow on Lana's tall, lean frame the eclectic outfit worked. While her cheeks had lost their twenty-something baby fat, her hair was the same mass of shiny black curls I remembered from college, and her green eyes sparkled with genuine pleasure as she came in for a big hug.

"Ohmigod, Maddie, it's been too long," she said, enveloping me in an embrace that smelled like peaches.

"Agreed," I said, returning the hug. "You look great."

Lana grinned. "Thanks. This whole outfit is from a new collection I'm designing. Even the shoes," she said, modeling the clogs.

"They are certainly one-of-a-kind," I said truthfully.

Lana ushered us into her private office in the back of the store, offering us seats on a comfortable velvet sofa and cups of herbal tea. After we caught each other up with the cliff-notes versions of what we'd been doing since college, I got down to the point of our visit.

"We wanted to ask you about the *Dancing with Celebrities* set," I said.

Lana nodded solemnly. "What a tragedy, right? Poor Irina."

"I don't suppose you noticed anything odd going on that day?" Dana asked. "Anyone on the set that didn't belong there or anything different in Irina's demeanor?"

"No." Lana looked at Dana, squinting her eyes for a moment. "You're Ricky's girlfriend, right?" she asked.

Dana bit her lower lip but nodded.

"I thought so. I knew I recognized you." She paused suddenly looking uncertain what to say next. Hallmark didn't exactly make a sympathy card for those whose boyfriends cheated on them then killed the other woman to cover up the crime. "I'm so sorry. This all must be very difficult for you," she finally settled on.

Dana cleared her throat, looking about as uncomfortable as Lana. "Thanks" she said.

"You were on set the day she..." Lana trailed off.

"We were actually there to see you," I told her.

"Me?" Lana's eyebrows rose. "Why?"

"We heard you'd had some wardrobe items stolen."

"Right. The thefts." Lana's back stiffened, and I could see a distinct shift in her mood.

"Can you tell us about them?"

Lana cleared her throat. "Well, it seems minor now in the face of..." She trailed off gesturing Dana's way. "You know. But, what did you want to know?"

"When was the first one?" I asked.

Lana looked off into space for a moment, searching the archives of her brain. "Last week. It was the shoes Irina had worn the week before in the tango number. Purple, strappy, rhinestones on the sides."

"So it was Irina's costume that went missing?" I jumped on the link.

Lana paused. "Well, hers was the first. But the missing items weren't limited to her things."

Drat. There went my connection.

"Anyway, the shoes weren't a big deal, since she'd already performed in that costume, and you know no costume gets used twice. But it was kind of annoying, you know? Like, I knew I had put them with the rest of the pieces, but suddenly they were gone."

"You said this was the first. What happened next?" Dana asked.

"Well, a few days later, after Kaylie did her waltz number, her headpiece was gone."

"Another item that had already been worn," I noted.

She nodded. "But the next time it was worse. A full gown that Shaniqua was scheduled to wear that week. It was missing right before dress rehearsals."

"That was when production had to shut down for a day," I added, remembering the story Felix had told me.

"Exactly! The producers were so pissed." I could see color staining Lana's cheeks at the memory. As much as she called the thefts minor now, I could tell they had caused her to get majorly upset at the time.

"But you found the gown finally?"

"Yes. Thank God!"

"Where was it?"

"It was shoved on a rack with a couple of Ricky's old costumes that were scheduled to be recycled."

"Is it possible it was just misplaced?" I asked, trying to be as delicate as possible about asking if it had just been a simple mistake on her part.

But Lana shook her head vehemently from side to side, her black curls bouncing around her shoulders. "No. That's what the producers thought, too. But it wasn't me. I can tell you that for sure! I'm not so careless as to recycle a current costume."

"Do you have any idea who else could have moved the costume?" I asked.

Lana shrugged. "I wish I did."

"What about the other items?" Dana jumped in. "Did you ever recover them?"

Lana shook her head. "No. But, like I said, we didn't look very hard. They'd already been used on the show, so we really didn't have much use for them. They were going to be recycled in the costume department." Lana paused. "We rip old costumes apart and use the pieces for new ones on other productions. The sequins and jewels from the dresses get repurposed. The shoes get re-dyed and reused elsewhere. Pretty much everything is salvageable, and what isn't gets donated to charity."

I cringed thinking that had almost happened to a current outfit. Considering how much those gowns must cost, I could see why the producers were upset about almost losing one.

"Anything else go missing after the gown?" I asked.

Lana shook her head. "No. After the gown someone leaked the story of the set being shut down," she said, frowning deeply. "As if the producers weren't pissed enough at me, I had the press hounding me then, too. I mean, it wasn't *my* fault someone was stealing from the set."

And that's when Felix had called me.

"Speaking of the *Informer*," I jumped in, "we passed one of their reporters leaving your shop just now."

Lana nodded. "Vultures. But at least they aren't hounding me anymore." She paused, shooting an apologetic look at Dana. "Sorry."

Dana nodded, that uncomfortable look returning.

"What did the reporter want to know?" I asked Lana.

"She wanted to know what I knew about Ricky and Irina."

Dana squared her chin. "It's okay. I can take it," she promised. "What do you know?"

Lana swallowed. "Okay. Well, she wanted to know if I'd seen them together. Seen them talking or hanging out together outside of rehearsals. That sort of thing."

"And had you?" Dana squeaked out.

Lana suddenly found a piece of lint on her skirt fascinating. "I'm afraid so," she said softly.

I felt Dana's heart hit the floor beside me. "What did you see?" she asked.

Lana licked her lips, shooting a gaze at Dana. "Well... there have been a couple of times when I saw Irina going into Ricky's dressing room," she started.

Dana paled a shade beneath her hastily applied foundation.

"But that wasn't unusual, right?" I quickly asked. "I mean, I'm sure the stars on the show were hanging out in each others' rooms all the time, right?"

Lana nodded slowly. "Sure." She paused. And from the way her eyes were shooting from me to Dana and down to that non-existent piece of lint again, I had a bad feeling that there was more she wasn't saying.

"But?" Dana asked.

Lana sucked in her cheek, eyes darting between us at a rapid speed. "Look, I didn't want to say anything to that reporter, because Ricky's a nice guy, and I really want to give him the benefit of the doubt here."

That bad feeling multiplied. "What did you not say to the reporter?" I asked.

I felt Dana steeling herself for the worst.

Lana sighed. She looked up at Dana again. "I'm so sorry. But the last time I saw Irina and Ricky going into his dressing room together was the day she died."

I felt my stomach clench, dread pooling into a puddle there. "When was this?"

Lana licked her lips, as if she didn't want to say it any more than Dana wanted to hear it. "Just a few minutes before they found her."

CHAPTER EIGHT

It took a trip to Pizza Hut for a large pepperoni and sausage, a drive through McDonald's for a bag of greasy fries, and a detour to Baskin Robbins before Dana stopped hyperventilating and looked somewhat like a normal person again.

"You gonna be okay?" I asked.

"I'm fine," she reassured me, around a bite of banana split that leaked out the corners of her mouth.

Not exactly convincing, but at least she wasn't breathing into a paper bag anymore.

"Lana just must have been mistaken," Dana said, forking another spoonful of chocolate and banana heaven into her mouth. I watched, my taste buds yearning with all their might for the sweet caress of ice cream.

"It's possible," I hedged.

"I mean, there is no way Ricky could have hurt Irina."

I noticed she didn't speak to the issue of him sleeping with her.

"I agree," I said, also avoiding the other issue. "Ricky did not kill Irina." I paused. "But I don't think Lana's a liar either."

Dana paused, spoonful of ice cream midway to her mouth, dripping little dots of dessert onto the Formica countertop. God, they looked good.

She took a deep breath. "Okay. Fine. Ricky was... with Irina before she died." She shoved the ice cream into her mouth, as if it might cleanse away the taste of what she'd just said.

"Right."

"But," she added, "I know he didn't kill her. He must have left her alive."

"I think, maybe you should talk to Ricky," I said slowly. "We have a witness who puts him with Irina. That really doesn't look good."

Dana looked pained. "Can you do it?"

"Me?" I squeaked out. "Why me? He's *your* boyfriend."

"Maddie, I just can't face him right now. I mean, what if he says…" she paused, tears forming behind her eye. "What if he admits it? I mean, not the killing, but, you know. The other thing. I just can't take it. Please. You have to do this for me?"

I opened my mouth to respond, but luckily was saved by my cell ringing in my pocket. I whipped it out to see Marco's name on my caller ID.

"What's up?" I answered.

"You haven't seen the *Informer* website have you?"

Uh-oh. "Not lately… why?"

"Because Dana is plastered across the front page. In a pair of Crocs!"

I closed my eyes and thought a really dirty word.

"How could you let her go outside in those?" Marco chastised me.

"She's having a bad day."

"Yeah, well it's about to get worse. The whole salon is talking about it! Everyone is speculating that she's off the deep end, losing her marbles, pulling a Britney!"

"We'll be right there."

* * *

Half an hour later I'd pulled Dana away from her comfort food, and we were in the famous golden triangle of Beverly Hills, pushing through the front doors of Fernando's salon.

Fernando was my step-father, or as I'd affectionately dubbed him, Faux Dad. The nickname was not only because he was a step, but also because just about everything about him was faux. His real name was Ralph, and he'd enjoyed a very modest upbringing in the Midwest before reinventing himself Cali style.

"Fernando" had a Spanish ancestry that could be traced back to Isabella, a year-round spray tan, and an accent that teetered on the border between Spain, Italy, and San Francisco. (Before he married Mom, I'd been at least fifty-percent sure he was gay.) If he was going to make it in this town, Faux Dad was smart enough to know it was all about image. And make it he had, boasting one of the most successful salons in the city, playing host not only to countless real housewives of Beverly Hills but also a couple of the ones from TV.

In keeping with the current trend of the moment, Fernando's was decorated in a sixties mod style, complete with big, plastic pod chairs in reception, large, orange paisley flocked wallpaper, and portraits of Jackie O in big, black frames amidst hand painted daisies and retro polka dots. The main reception desk was a clear, plastic thing with a slab of polished wood on top and Marco sitting behind it.

As soon as we pushed through the glass front doors, he pounced. "Ohmigod, ohmigod, it's true!" he shouted, sucking in a breath as he got a look at Dana's footwear.

Her cheeks went pink. "I've had a bad day," she protested in defense.

Marco clucked his tongue. "Honey, no one's day is that bad."

"Show me the website," I insisted, coming around the reception desk to his computer.

Marco did, pulling up the *Informer*'s site as we looked over his shoulder. Splashed across the homepage beneath the "Fashion Victim of the Day" tagline was an image of Dana on the sidewalk outside The Sunshine State: sweats hanging limply on her hips, tank stretched out on one side, hair frizzing in the humidity as it escaped from her messy bun, feet stuck into the finest in plastics.

I thought some more dirty words aimed at one perky tabloid reporter. Allie hadn't been holding her phone up *just* to check the time on it. She'd also snapped the most unflattering photo of Dana that I had ever seen. That sneaky little...

My friend must have agreed as I heard her gasp beside me, hands flying to her mouth.

"Ohmigod, do I really look like that?"

I bit my lip trying to come up with a kind response. "It's been a bad day," I settled on again.

"My image is ruined," Dana wailed, thunking her head on Marco's desk. "My career is ruined. What am I going to do?"

"Well, for starters, we're gonna do something about this," Marco said, lifting a lock of frizzy strawberry blonde hair off his keyboard. "Honey, you need a hot oil treatment, stat!"

Dana nodded dumbly. "Okay."

"Then we'll talk about those Crocs once you've had some fashion sense pedicured back into you."

* * *

While Dana was in the very capable hands of Marco, I sat in reception and made a couple of calls. The first was to Felix, which went straight to voicemail.

"Call off your perky little pit-bull," I told him. "Dana's going through enough. She doesn't need to be a front page crime of fashion." I paused. While I knew Felix lived for the story - and this was definitely a juicy one - I tried to appeal to his human side. I was 90% sure he had one. "Please," I added. Then hung up.

The second call was to Ricky, which also went straight to voicemail. If I didn't know better, I would say people were screening me.

"Hey, it's Maddie. Listen, we need to talk. Dana's a wreck." I paused. "Just check the *Informer* site for proof of that. Anyway, I'm driving up to see you. I'll be there in..." I looked down at my watch. It was nearing 3:00pm, the witching hour when L.A. freeways magically turned from travel routes to parking lots. "...forty-five minutes," I finished, optimistically.

I hung up, checked in on Dana (who was encased in hot oil for her hair, paraffin treatments for both hands and feet, and a soothing cucumber face mask while awaiting a full body salt rub), texted Mom to see how the twins were doing (who promptly texted back that everyone was "just ducky"), and headed toward the PCH before traffic became tragic.

Malibu was about thirty miles north of L.A. proper, accessible by the Pacific Coast Highway, which snaked scenically along the coast, playing host to miles of white sand, funky seafood restaurants, and surf shacks. While the city was virtually inaccessible during rush hour, you weren't anyone in Hollywood until you had a beach house getaway on a cliff overlooking the ocean in Malibu. And Ricky was certainly someone. Which, as it turned out, was a good thing, because if there was ever a time he needed to get away, this was it.

Predictably, the winding drive to Ricky's place was packed with paparazzi. News vans mingled with the beat up Hyundai's of freelancers, all of them pointing wide-angle lenses at the house on the off chance that Ricky made an appearance. I had to drive half a block away just to find a spot to park, then I mentally crossed my fingers that Ricky would even see me as I trudged back to his front gates and hit the intercom. I felt curious paparazzi closing in, snapping photos as the system buzzed to life.

"No interviews," came the response through the speaker.

"Maddie Springer," I said. "I'm a friend of Ricky's. Can you please tell him I'm here?" I asked the unseen security guard.

I heard a beep and a buzz, which I hoped was the guard signing off to go find Ricky.

I shifted from foot to foot, feeling the intense stares of the paparazzi grow more interested the longer I stood there. I crossed my arms over my chest, trying not to look as self-conscious as I felt.

I waited a full five minutes, before I spotted a sleek, black car coming down the drive toward the gates.

The paparazzi jumped to attention, flashes going off like fireworks. The car stopped at the gate, and a guy in a black suit, sunglasses, and an earpiece that looked like it had been swiped from the Secret Service got out. The flashes immediately ceased, a collective groan from the media signaling their disappointment that it wasn't Ricky.

Secret Service Guy opened the gate and motioned me through, giving dirty looks to the paparazzi outside. I slipped past him and got into the passenger seat of the car, riding in silence as the bodyguard drove me up to the main house. As soon as we arrived, the guard ushered me through the front door and into a wide hall. "Ricky's in there," he grunted, gesturing to a room at my right.

I walked through a pair of French double doors, taking in the décor as I did.

While Dana had invited me several times to the place she and Ricky shared in the Hollywood Hills, I'd actually never been to the Malibu getaway. Cool white marble tiled the floors, and white walls with pale wood accents gave the home a modern feel. Bright paintings done by some famous artist lined the walls, but it was the scenery stretching outside of the oversized windows that had me catching my breath. Turquoise blue sea, rugged green cliff sides, and soft, sandy beaches.

"Cool, huh?" Ricky said, getting up from a chair in the corner as I approached.

I nodded. "Very cool. To die for," I added. Then silently cursed my poor choice of words. "How are you holding up?"

Ricky shrugged, doing a small, self-deprecating smile. "Been better, but I'll be okay."

He was unshaven, barefoot, and wearing a rumpled t-shirt and basketball shorts. It was a far cry from the Red Carpet Ricky his fans knew.

"Dana's not with you, huh?" he asked, his eyes darting behind me.

I shook my head and thought I saw his shoulders slump in response. "Sorry."

"Have a seat," he said, gesturing to a white leather sofa.

I did. "She's pretty upset, Ricky," I told him.

He nodded. "I know. And I'm so, so sorry. You have to believe that I never meant to hurt her."

"Give it to me straight," I told him. "What was going on between you and Irina?"

"Nothing," he said quickly. A little too quickly.

"Ricky, she was seen going into your dressing room. More than once," I added, remembering both Kaylie's and Lana's accounts.

"We were friends."

"That's it?"

"That's it. I swear."

I bit my lip. As much as I wanted to believe him, it was clear that he was holding something back. "Ricky, Lana saw you going into your dressing room with Irina just before she was found dead."

His skin paled beneath his five o-clock shadow. He leaned forward, hands clasped in front of him as if in an unconscious pleading motion. "Maddie, I did not kill her."

"So what were you two doing in there?"

"Talking," he said, his eyes suddenly avoiding mine.

For such a great actor, he was a terrible liar.

"Ricky, she was naked."

He shook his head. "No, she was clothed when she was with me. I swear it. I went into my dressing room with her. We... talked... then I left."

"You left her in your dressing room?"

He bit his lip, looking past me out toward the ocean as if it held the correct answer. Finally he nodded. "I was coming right back. I just had to... to get something."

"What something?"

"I... it was... look, that doesn't matter," he said, shaking his head. "What matters is she was alive and fully clothed when I left her."

Oh, yeah. He was definitely hiding something. I narrowed my eyes at him, trying to figure out what. "What time was that?" I asked.

"I... I don't remember. It wasn't like I was looking at my watch."

"Where did you go?"

His eyes ducked down, avoiding mine again. "Around. On the set."

"That's about the worst alibi I've ever heard."

"I'm not guilty," he shot back. "I wasn't planning on needing an alibi."

"Were you alone?"

"Yes," he said, eyes shifting downward.

"And no one saw you leave the dressing room?"

"No."

"Or saw Irina alive after you left her?"

"No." He paused. "Except the *real* killer."

"You do realize how O.J. that sounds, right?" I asked him.

"Look, I didn't kill her, Maddie," he said, eyes pleading with me. "You have to believe me."

"Did Irina ever mention a Russian guy?" I asked him, switching gears. "Average height, dark hair, wears a diamond earring in one ear?"

Ricky frowned. "No. Not that I remember. Why? Who is he?"

"I wish I knew. Shaniqua says she overheard Irina plotting with this man to buy votes for the show."

Ricky's eyes went wide. "No way!"

"Way. She didn't tell you anything about it?"

He shook his head vehemently. "No. I had no idea she would do that. I mean, why would she need to? We were ahead every week. I honestly thought we had a pretty good shot at the prize."

"So did I," I admitted. "But apparently, Irina wanted to make sure."

"So, you think this Russian guy might have killed her?" Ricky asked, hope lighting his eyes.

I shrugged. "I'm looking into it."

Ricky smiled. "Thanks, Maddie. You have no idea how much it means to me that you believe in me."

I grunted a non-committal response back. Mostly because I didn't have the heart to tell him my belief was wavering.

* * *

Once I got home, I took one pair of happy, giggling babies from Mom and thanked her for her help.

Unfortunately, as soon as I shut the front door behind her both twins started crying.

"Don't worry, Mommy's here," I cooed to them, picking Max up. Which somehow prompted him to cry even harder.

I tried not to take it personally as I filled the kitchen sink with water, stripped the poor things out of their duck suits, and gave the pair a bath in their little recliner tubs. The warm water eventually soothed them, allowing me to dress, feed, burp and change (and, in Olivia's case, *re-change*) them before I finally wore them out, and they fell asleep in their matching cribs. I was just tiptoeing out of the nursery with baby monitor in hand when Ramirez came through the front door.

"Hey, I'm home," he called.

"Shh," I commanded, pointing to the monitor.

"Oops. Sorry," he whispered. "I missed them, huh?" I could see genuine disappointment in his eyes.

"Yeah, they just went down."

He nodded. "How'd they do today?"

"Great," I said. Or at least, that's what I'd been told.

"Good. Maybe I'll try to slip home at lunch tomorrow and get some play time in."

I nodded. "I'm sure they'd like that." I made a mental note to be here at lunch time.

"How was your day?" I asked. I'll admit, I had a twofold agenda with that question. Of course I cared how my husband's day went, but I also cared if he'd encountered any new leads on the case that was taking me in circles to nowhere fast.

"It was good," he said, taking off his jacket and laying it over the back of the sofa before plopping down. "Busy, but good."

"Busy with..." I prodded, taking a seat beside him.

He grinned. "Irina's case, and you know it."

"So, how's the case going?"

"You're incorrigible," he said, grinning as he put one arm around my shoulders.

I leaned into his chest, inhaling the faint scent of aftershave still clinging to his shirt. No matter how long we were together, the smell never ceased to turn me on.

"I know," I responded. "But you love me anyway."

"Most days."

"Hey!" I punched him playfully in the ribs.

He chuckled. "Okay, okay, since you've been stuck at home all day with the terrible two, I'll throw you a bone."

"Thank you," I said, even though a flush of guilt hit my cheeks at being just the teeny tiniest bit deceptive about how I'd spent my day.

"Irina's autopsy was today," he went on.

"And?"

"And we got more info on the murder weapon that killed her."

"So what was it?" I asked.

Ramirez shrugged. "Honestly, we're still not sure. But it was a heavy, blunt instrument."

I felt my shoulders sag. "That was hardly a bone."

"But," he added, "it left a distinct impression on her skull."

I perked back up. "What kind of impression?"

"Triangular. About this big," he said, holding his thumb and forefinger a couple of inches apart. "With a cross hatched pattern on it."

"Any guesses what made it?"

Ramirez shook his head. "Unfortunately, nothing left at the scene seems to match the pattern."

"And I assume none of your fancy police databases had any hits?"

He shook his head. "We're still looking, though. Anyway, enough work talk," he said. "What's for dinner?"

I shrugged. "Whatever you're in the mood to make me."

Ramirez groaned. "I was afraid of that. I guess it's sandwiches again."

"Or," I said, a tiny light bulb going off. "We could go out. There's this new place I've been dying to try. Tapas Mexicana?"

"Sounds like a lot of work hauling two sleeping babies with us," Ramirez protested, putting his feet up on the coffee table.

"Well, since they're asleep already, they're probably good to go for at least a couple of hours before they wake up hungry. I could see if Dana wants to come over and hang here with them while we go eat."

"I don't know. I've been out all day..."

"Oh, come on. We haven't had a date night in forever. Just the two of us? It will be fun." I gave him my brightest smile, hoping he bought it.

Ramirez sighed, clearly weighing his options. But considering he'd been living on sandwiches for the last two days, his stomach finally won over his tired feet. "Okay, Springer. You win. Date night it is."

CHAPTER NINE

———

Half an hour later Dana was sitting on my sofa watching reruns of *CSI* on demand while waiting for a delivery of mu shu pork, spring rolls, lemon chicken, chow fun, and egg fried rice from the Shanghi Palace. And once I told her about my meeting with Ricky, she added a cheesecake to her list of demands. If her body didn't go into junk-food shock by the end of the night, it would be a miracle. On the upside, after the afternoon at Fernando's she was looking more like her movie star self. Even if said self was still shoved into a pair of sweats. (Minus the Crocs. Marco told me he'd tossed them in the dumpster out back as soon as he could get his hands on them, sending her home in salon issued flip-flops instead.)

I left Dana with the remote and the number to a bakery that delivered 24/7 (a fav of mine in my pre-baby-weight life), and, after a quick jaunt through traffic, Ramirez and I were walking through the doors of Tapas Mexicana. The place was small, as all popular restaurants in L.A. seemed to be, but it was intimate rather than cramped feeling. Tables for two lined the walls, soft acoustic guitar music played through hidden speakers, and the air smelled like chili powder, cumin, and cinnamon. I inhaled deeply, wondering if just one little night off my diet was really all that bad.

As the host showed us to our table, I surveyed the other patrons. A handful of guys in suits - network exec types. A few in jeans and sneakers - writer types, trying to cozy up to the exec types. And several blondes in tops tight enough to show off their surgically enhanced girls - actress types trying to get the attention of all the other types. And amidst the attention seekers, there was one rumpled looking tabloid editor type, seated at a table near the center of the room, his back to me, leaning toward a blonde in a little black dress. (Emphasis on "little".)

"Oh look who it is," I said, grabbing Ramirez by the arm and feigning surprise. "Felix Dunn!"

Ramirez squinted toward the table in question, then grunted. "Swell."

To say Ramirez and Felix had a tenuous relationship was like saying Christina Aguilera wore a *little* makeup. Total understatement alert. Ramirez and I had just started dating when I first met Felix. At the time, Felix had been hot on a story involving yours truly, which hadn't exactly endeared him to me. However, as I'd gotten to know Felix, I'd realized there was more to him than just his tabloid boy facade. And, admittedly, I'd softened to him. So soft that at one time I might have even kissed him. In the heat of the moment. Accidentally. Totally not meaning to. But I hadn't exactly hated it either.

You can imagine how Ramirez had reacted. In fact, his feelings toward Felix, and my own heat-of-the-moment-whoops, had almost derailed our relationship for good. But, in the end, I'd gone with my heart and pledged my undying love and sole possession of my lips to Ramirez. Leaving things between Felix and me in the land of what-if, and almost-was.

Not that it meant Ramirez had forgotten it all.

Especially if the look on his face that accompanied the grunt was any indication. If I'd said, "Look honey, Jack the Ripper is here," he'd have probably been more enthused.

But, as it was, that Ripper was dining with the one person who had "gory details" about my case. And I planned to find out exactly what they were.

"Can we sit near our friends?" I asked the host, pointing toward Felix's table.

Ramirez turned on me, eyes narrowed, suspicion radar rising.

I did my best eyelash-batting-wide-eyed-innocence thing.

Luckily, there was a free table, just two over from Felix and Allie.

Unluckily, Ramirez continued giving me The Look as the host led us to it. I tried to ignore it, though it was like ignoring laser beams being shot into my back.

"Did you know he was going to be here?" Ramirez grunted into my ear.

"No!" I did a "puh-sha" thing, expelling air through my teeth. "I mean, why would I want to meet up with him for our date night?"

Ramirez just grunted again, his eyes narrowing further.

And his weren't the only ones.

Allie spotted us as we approached. Her eyeliner heavy eyes first went round with surprise, then narrowed into a matching pair to my husbands'.

"Maddie." She said my name as it if were a dirty word.

"Why, Allie!" I responded, laying the sugar on double-iced. "What a surprise to see you here."

She pursed her lips together. "Really."

I ignored her. "And Felix, so nice to see you."

Felix swiveled in his chair, the only person in the group not shooting me daggers at the moment. "Maddie, don't you look lovely tonight?"

"Thank you, I try."

Ramirez grunted again.

"And Jackson," Felix said, acknowledging the grunter. "Lovely to see you as always." He stuck a hand out in a friendly gesture. Ramirez grabbed it so hard I feared he'd crush it.

"Well, I don't want to interrupt your dinner," I said, steering my husband away as Felix extracted his hand, only wincing slightly. "Enjoy your meal," I added, then quickly skirted over to our own table. I took a seat and grabbed a menu, propping it in front of my face to shield me from the laser beams still being trained at me from across the table.

I only got as far as the salad section before my husband's hand shot out and lowered my shield.

"Maddie." He said my name low, dark, and in the dangerous tone I knew he used to interrogate suspects.

I gulped and pulled out Innocent Face again. "Yes, dear?"

"What was that?" he asked pointedly.

"What was what, honey?"

"That. With Felix and Allie."

I blinked again. "What?"

More eye-narrowing. It was a wonder he could see out of those suckers at all.

"What?" I protested. "I can't say hello to a friend who I *happen* to run into at a restaurant."

"'Happen?'"

I set my menu down on the table. "Just what are you suggesting, Ramirez?"

"What I'm suggesting, *Springer*, is that it's a hell of a coincidence."

I shrugged. "It's a small town. Coincidences happen."

He crossed his arms over his chest. "It's not *that* small."

"Look, do you want to grill me, or do you want to order a bottle of wine and enjoy the one night out we've managed to have in the last three months?" I asked.

Ramirez grunted again, but he picked up his menu and started reading, which I took as a good sign. Crisis averted.

Now, to get what I'd really come here for.

The server appeared, we ordered a bottle of Pinot and a selection of appetizer-sized tapas plates, and Ramirez dug into the bowl of chips in front of us. I followed suit, my eyes focused on the food while my ears tried to pick up any snippet of conversation I could from the table two over where Allie was giving Felix an earful about something. Something important if the little frown between her threaded brows was any indication.

I wished we'd been sitting next to them. The couple between our tables was older, casually dressed, and talking about their youngest child who, if the gist of the conversation I overheard was any indication, was spending a fortune at college.

I tried to tune them out, honing in instead on Allie's mouth as she formed the words.

"... together on *Dancing with Celebrities*.... overheard the name... very reliable source... *and then he went and charged an entire week's hotel stay in Ft. Lauderdale over spring break.*"

I paused, shaking my head as the older woman's voice rose in volume. I didn't care about the spring break kid. I cared about what name was overheard on DWC.

I cocked my head to the side, straining to hear over the couple again. This time it was Felix talking.

"You're sure your source is being straight with you?"

"Absolutely. 100% trustworthy," Allie responded.

I knew it! There *was* a press leak on DWC. And he or she was leaking info straight to Allie. I strained, hoping to hear a name.

"And your source saw them together before Irina died?" Felix asked.

I saw Allie nod, her blonde bangs bobbing up and down. "Right before she... *said to the captain that I could use the overtime anyway - earth to Maddie?*"

"What?" I snapped my attention back to my husband, realizing he'd been talking.

"Are you even listening to me?" Ramirez asked, frowning.

"What? Yes. Of course."

"Oh really?" He crossed his arms over his chest. "What was I saying then?"

"You were saying.... something about your captain..." I bit my lip. Then I crossed *my* arms over *my* chest. "You know what? It's just insulting that you're even questioning my ability to listen to you."

Ramirez's eyes took on that dark, dangerous, staring-down-a-perp-in-a-holding-cell look again. "Okay, that's it. What's really going on here?"

"What's going on," I said, trying to hold onto my mock indignity for all it was worth, "is that I'm trying to have a lovely date night with my husband who has clearly been spending too much time at work because he's all suspicion and narrowy eyes," I said, gesturing to the eyes in question. Which, by the way, did not let up any.

"Furthermore-" I went on.

Ramirez raised an eyebrow my way. "'Furthermore?' What are you a PBS character?"

My turn to narrow my eyes. "*Furthermore*, I will not sit here and be accused of... well, whatever it is you're accusing me of."

Ramirez's arms were still crossed, but I could see the hint of a smile curving the corner of his mouth. "You done, Springer?"

"Yes." I paused, watching Allie get up from her table and head toward the back of the restaurant. "I mean, no. I... have to pee. And when I get back, I hope we can have a nice, adult meal without any more accusations." I punctuated the last bit by throwing my napkin down and grabbing my purse as I hightailed it after Allie.

I didn't dare look back. I was 100% sure Ramirez was staring after me. And only 50% sure he'd believed my performance.

I quickly rounded the corner of the dining room, making my way down a short hallway that lead to the restrooms. I pushed into the sanctuary of the ladies' room and spotted Allie's stilettos peeking out from under one of the stalls.

I waited for her at the mirror, pulling out a tube of lip-gloss, reapplying my Raspberry Perfection. Finally I heard a tell-tale flush, the stall door opened, and Allie walked out, making for the sink beside me.

"Okay, what's the deal, Maddie?" she asked as she washed her hands. "What are you doing here?"

"Just touching up my make-up," I answered.

"I mean at the restaurant," she said, turning on me. "You knew I was going to be here with Felix. What are you trying to do?"

"Fine," I relented. "I want to know what you know about Irina's death."

Allie stared me down. "So why not just ask me?"

"Okay. What do you know about Irina's death?"

"Lots." She grinned. "And you can read all about it in the *Informer* next week."

I gritted my teeth. "Look, Ricky is a friend of mine. A good friend. I know he didn't do this."

Allie paused. "A *good* friend, huh?"

I nodded. "Very."

She grinned, a big, wicked Cheshire cat thing. "Okay then, I'll make you a deal."

Uh-oh. I had a bad feeling making a deal with Allie was like making a deal with the devil's perkier little sister. "What kind of deal?"

"I'll share what I know about Irina."

"I like it so far," I hedged.

"In exchange for an interview with Ricky."

"Ha!" The expletive blasted from me before I could stop it. "No way would Ricky go for that. You called him Dancing Death."

"Oh come on! You know I couldn't ignore a headline story like that."

"And you featured Dana as the Fashion Victim of the Day!"

"Okay, she brought that on herself. She was wearing Crocs. In public."

I had to agree with her there. "Be that as it may, you're not exactly Ricky's favorite person at the moment."

"But you're *very* good friends with him, right? You could persuade him to be a little more friendly toward me."

"There's persuade, then there's move mountains."

A tiny frown settled between Allie's brows. "Fine," she said. "Then you're on your own."

She flipped her blonde hair over one shoulder and turned back to her reflection in the mirror, making a big show of ignoring me as she pulled out a tube of ruby red lipstick.

I scrunched my nose up. I bit my lip. I closed my eyes. "Fine."

Allie's head whipped around faster than a tilt-a-whirl. "Fine?"

"Fine, I'll talk to Ricky."

Her face lit up like Christmas, and she emitted a squeal only small Chihuahuas could hear.

"But I can't promise anything," I warned. "Like I said, Ricky pretty much hates your guts."

"But you'll talk to him?" Allie asked, her eyes shining. "You'll persuade him to do an interview?"

I bit my lip. "I'll do my best."

She giggled and clapped like a twelve-year-old.

"Okay, so spill it," I demanded. "What do you know about Irina?"

"Irina was seen with a woman named Katrina last week on the *Dancing with Celebrities* set," Allie told me.

I shrugged. "So? Who's Katrina?"

"According to sources, she's someone who looks exactly like Irina."

"Exactly as in..."

"Twins."

"So, Irina has a sister," I mused, the information opening up new possibilities.

"Not only that," Allie said, "but they were arguing."

I raised one eyebrow her way. "Arguing as in you-borrowed-my-fav-shoes-without-asking or as in I'm-gonna-bludgeon-you-to-death?"

Allie shrugged. "All I know is it was heated and just days before Irina died."

"How do you know all this?"

Allie shrugged. "A little birdie told me."

"The same little birdie who's also been leaking you stories about theft, murder, and Ricky's whereabouts," I confirmed. "Who is it?"

But Allie wagged a finger at me. "Ah, ah, ah. A good reporter never reveals her sources."

While the jury was still out on the type of human being Allie was, she was, admittedly, a good reporter.

"Fine. What else *can* you tell me?"

Allie shook her head. "Sorry, that's it." She puckered doing a kissy face at herself in the mirror.

"What about an address for Katrina? Where can I find her?"

"When you get Ricky to agree to the interview, maybe I can share more."

I narrowed my eyes at her. I wasn't sure how much she was bluffing or how much more she really did know, but if she was holding out on me...

"This isn't a game, Allie," I warned her.

"No kidding," she agreed. "Which is why you should leave the investigating to the real investigators."

"You're a tabloid reporter," I pointed out.

"*Investigative* reporter," she corrected. "Which qualifies me to run with this case a lot more than someone who *used to be* a fashion designer."

I narrowed my eyes at her. "I *am* a fashion designer."

"Oh yeah? When was the last time you actually designed a shoe?"

I opened my mouth to respond, but realized I had no good answer for that. Mostly because I couldn't remember.

"Trust me, I will get to the truth," Allie assured me. "And the best way you can help is to get me that interview with Ricky." She capped her lipstick and made another kissy-face in the mirror at herself. "Enjoy your meal," she called as she skipped out of the bathroom.

* * *

Instead of enjoying my meal, I spent the rest of it deep in thought, wondering what the argument between the sisters had been about, whether it had anything to do with one of them turning up dead, and where our mystery man with the diamond earring fit into all of it. And then if maybe everyone was right and I should just stay home with the twins and leave the investigating to the investigators. I mean, Allie *had* found out a lot more about Irina than I had. And Ramirez *did* have more resources than I did. And Ricky *did* have the best lawyer money could buy. Did he really even need me?

I was so distracted by those thoughts that I even accidentally ordered fried ice cream for dessert. (Yes it was a total accident, not my willpower crapping out on me. That's my story and I'm sticking to it.) Unfortunately, by the time we got home and saw Dana off, I was no closer to coming to any conclusions about anything.

"So how was our favorite tabloid reporter tonight?" Ramirez asked, reaching for a bottle of wine from the rack by the fridge.

"Hmm?" I asked, shaking myself out of my thoughts.

"Allie. You two did have a girl's moment in the restroom, right?"

"Uh…" I paused, wondering just how much of our "girl's moment" he might have guessed at. "Sort of?" I said, ending the statement in a distinct question mark.

Ramirez's eyes softened. "Look, I understand now why you wanted to go to that restaurant and talk to Allie."

I froze, wineglass halfway to my lips. "You do?"

"Sure. Dana's your friend. I'd be pissed if someone printed a pic of a friend looking like hell, too."

"Wait – you read the *Informer*?"

Ramirez grinned. "Someone left the screen open this afternoon."

"Right." I took a sip. Mostly to cover my relief that Ramirez thought my reason for confronting Allie was purely press related and not having to do with any investigating that I was *not* doing.

"Anyway," he said. "I hope you set her straight."

I nodded noncommittally, taking another covering sip. "Sorry I used date night as a cover to see her," I said, honestly meaning it.

Ramirez grinned, his eyes going dark and devilish. "Tell you what. I can think of one way you can make it up to me," he took a step toward me.

"You can, huh?"

"Uh-huh." He put his arms around me, his lips grazing my neck.

I immediately went warm in all the right places. "You know, we've got at least an hour before Livvie wakes up for her midnight feeding," I pointed out.

Ramirez leaned in close, his breath warm and tingly on my ear. "Then I say we make the most of it."

* * *

I awoke to the sound of loud screeching in the vicinity of my nightstand. I fumbled with the baby monitor, my eyes blinking open to take in faint pre-dawn light filtering through the windows. It took me a moment to realize the high-pitched sound was not a twin but coming from my cell phone.

I grabbed it, stabbing the on button.

"Hello?" I croaked. Between the wine, the late night, my husband's talents (and, boy, did he have a lot of them), and two twin awakenings, I think I'd slept a total of two hours. And my voice sounded like it.

"Maddie!" I heard a voice on the other end shout.

"Dana?" I asked, recognition peeking through my sleepy haze.

"Ohmigod, it's a nightmare," her voice trembled.

I sat up, adrenaline kicking in. "What's a nightmare? What's going on? Are you okay?"

"Yes. No. Maybe. I don't know," she wailed. "I fell asleep with the TV on last night, and this morning I woke up and there it was."

"There what was?" I asked, reaching into my nightstand for the TV remote. I flipped it on, watching as the early morning crew on Channel Six filled the screen.

"Ricky," Dana said, even as the image of her boyfriend filled my screen, too. "Maddie, they've arrested him for murder!"

CHAPTER TEN

———

"How could you," I asked, swatting my husband on the arm.

"Uhn," he grunted, rolling over in bed as his eyes flickered open. "How could I what?"

"Arrest Ricky!" I yelled, gesturing to the TV screen where the movie star's image was being led away in handcuffs.

"Oh." He yawned loudly. "That."

I swatted him again. "Yes, *that*."

Ramirez sighed and propped himself up on his elbows. I clenched my jaw, refusing to let the sight of the sheets slipping down his toned, bare torso distract me. "That was low, Jack."

"Look, it wasn't my call," he said.

"But you could have said something! Warned me. Given Dana the heads-up so she didn't have to find out from Channel Six. You knew they were arresting him this morning, didn't you?"

Ramirez sighed again. Then nodded. "Yeah, I knew."

"Then whey didn't you warn me?"

"Because you would have warned Dana, and she would have warned Ricky," he continued. "And we couldn't risk him fleeing."

"Ricky would not flee. Ricky's innocent," I pointed out, not for the first time.

Ramirez shook his head at me. "I hate to break it to you, but it's not just guilty people who get scared and run."

I opened my mouth to protest that he would never do that to Dana, but I realized I wasn't 100% sure on that score. I mean, he *had* run off to Malibu to hide out. He had been with Irina just before she died. And it looked very much like he had cheated with her.

"Look," Ramirez said, "if Ricky is innocent-"

"He *is* innocent," I emphasized, ignoring the small wavering doubt whispering in the back of my mind.

"Sure." He nodded. Though I could tell by the look in his eyes that his wavering doubt had a distinctly louder voice than mine. "And if that's the case, the evidence will clear him."

I pursed my lips together. While Ramirez had less faith in our friend than I did, he had way more faith in the justice system than I did. With the number of celebrities that had gotten away with murder in this town, I had no doubt the cops would delight in making an example of Ricky.

Which meant we were now on borrowed time to get to the truth about Irina's death.

* * *

Two hours, four cups of coffee, and one aspirin later Ramirez was at the station processing Ricky, and Dana was at my front door, processing a venti mocha latte with extra whip and caramel syrup.

I was absolutely dying to join her, but I held onto my willpower in a two fisted death grip as I sipped my own coffee. Minus the cream. And sweetener. And flavor.

"I need chocolate," she said by way of greeting as she pushed through the front door, making a dash for my kitchen.

"You okay?" I asked.

"No. But I will be once I get a Hershey's bar." She opened a cupboard and scrunched up her nose at the contents. "God, all you have is diet food."

"I'm on a diet," I said weakly, sipping my bitter coffee.

She slumped into a kitchen chair. "I don't know what to do. I mean, should I visit him in jail? Should I stay away? Should I break up with him? Do you think he did it?"

"Killed Irina?" I asked, jumping on the easiest question first. "No." I was 90% sure.

"Do you think he cheated?"

I bit my lip, remembering the way he'd kept averting his eyes when I'd questioned him. "You want the honest answer or the comforting one."

She paused. "Honest."

"I think he-"

"No, wait! Comforting!" she cried.

I put an arm around her. "I think you need to lay off the junk food," I told her. Then I poured myself another cup of flavorless caffeine, and I told her about my conversation the night before with Allie.

"So, you think maybe Katrina killed her sister?" Dana asked when I was done.

"I think the argument is certainly worth looking into."

"Agreed," Dana said.

Which left only one dilemma - what to do with the babies.

I texted my usual go-to babysitters. Unfortunately, Mom sent me a text back saying she was getting a facial that morning. Ramirez's mom was doing a bake sale for the church. And Auntie Marco was busy putting together a party for an A-lister whose name he couldn't say. Though he dropped the hint that it started with a "Kar" and rhymed with "smashy-in".

I looked down at Livvie and Max as I hung up the phone on my last resort.

"It looks like we might have to take them with us," I said, throwing Dana an apologetic look.

But she just shrugged. "Fine. But let's hit the In-N-Out drive-thru first. I need a milkshake." She paused. "And a cheeseburger."

* * *

While I navigated the drive-thru, Dana pulled up Google on her phone and looked up the name "Katrina Sokolov".

As she read off the results to me (between mouthfuls of decadent burger that had my black-coffee digesting stomach growling like a caged tiger) one thing became instantly clear. According to the best Google had to offer, there was no Katrina Sokolov. In fact, there was no mention of Irina having a sister anywhere. Which was, in itself, suspicious. Irina must have worked hard to keep her off the press's radar.

From everything we could tell, it looked like there was just one person who even had knowledge of the existence of a twin sister.

Allie's informant.

I flipped a U-turn on Santa Monica, pointing the minivan toward the *Informer*'s offices.

The *L.A. Informer* was located in Hollywood, just two blocks east of the trendy part where tourists flocked to the Walk of Fame and two blocks west of the scary part where gangs would shoot you for wearing the wrong team jersey. It was housed on the second story of an old, stucco building that had a faded awning shading the front doors and a rusted fire escape clinging to the side for dear life. If anyone actually had to use it to escape, I feared it would disintegrate.

I parked the minivan in the lot around back and turned to peek at the twins. Both were sound asleep in their seats.

"You go," Dana whispered, gesturing to the building. "I'll stay here and watch them."

"You sure?" I asked.

She nodded. "It's probably safer that way."

She had a point. A celeb walking into the *Informer* offices was like a minnow swimming into a shark's den. Certain death. Or at least front page headlines. And considering Dana was wearing the dark circles of one who had slept almost as little as I had, and she had opted for another pair of comfy sweats today (though she'd thankfully upgraded to a pair of sparkly, wedged Mary-Jane sneakers), staying off the front page was probably in her best interest. So I left her with the sleeping beauties as I prepared to face the paparazzi on my own.

As soon as the elevator doors opened on the second floor, I was assaulted by the sounds of keyboards clacking, phones ringing, and a dozen voices all shouting over each other about exclusives and candid shots. The large space was divided with cubicle half-walls, which everyone seemed to ignore, shouting over the tops of them. In the center of the room sat one office, walled in with glass, and in the center of that sat Felix, his back to me, Bluetooth in one ear, arms waving madly. I charged toward him, ignoring the looks from curious cube-dwellers as I did. One thing I'll say for tabloid reporters - they didn't miss much.

"I don't care how private it is, I want wedding shots," I heard Felix shout into his headpiece as I entered his office.

He spun at the sound of my footsteps, nodding and waving me in.

"So hire our own helicopter," he shouted. "I don't care what it costs. (pause) Wait, it'll cost what?! (pause) Good God, I don't want to buy the helicopter, just rent it. (pause) Never mind. Pay off a guest with a cell instead. We don't need pro quality shots, just shots. I need that dress on the front page, understood?" he said, then punctuated it by hitting the off button and pulling the piece from his ear.

"Maddie, love, to what do I owe this pleasure?" he asked, coming in for a quick hug.

"Hi, Felix," I greeted him, returning it.

"Three times in one week, now," he said. "I'm beginning to think you can't stay away from me." He gave me a playful wink.

Despite the joking tone of his voice, I felt my cheeks warm. "Yes, well, I hate to bother you, but I need some help."

"Help with...?"

"Information about a celeb."

His eyebrows turned inward in a frown. "Which one?"

"Irina Sokolov."

The name did nothing to alleviate his wrinkle inducing expression. "May I ask why?"

"If I say 'no' will you still help me?"

He crossed his arms over his chest. "Not likely."

I sighed. "Okay. Look, Allie has an informant on the set of DWC. The informant knows something about Irina that may help Ricky's case. I need to speak to him. Or her," I amended.

"Allie's on assignment today. She's not here," Felix informed me.

"Perfect. Then you can tell me everything without her knowing."

He shot me a look. "I'm sorry, but Allie's informant is Allie's informant."

"Meaning?"

"Meaning I haven't the slightest clue who it is."

I opened my mouth to protest that he must have the *slightest* clue, but he cut me off before I had the chance.

"And even if I did, I wouldn't share it with you."

I shut my mouth with a click. "You wouldn't?" Despite any past we might have shared, he was making his current allegiance very clear.

"No. Look, I do value our friendship, Maddie," he said, obviously sensing my disappointment. "But it's journalism 1-0-1 to keep your informants' identities private."

I cocked my head to the side. "Seriously? Felix, you work at a tabloid. Nothing is private around you people. I think you printed a photo of Brad Pitt coming out of a public restroom last week."

"Yes, and you'll notice we didn't print who told us that Brad was at that particular restroom," he pointed out. "Whoever Allie is getting her information from, that's between her and them. And," he added, "I trust Allie to follow up on that information. She knows her job, and she's good at it."

That I didn't doubt. What I doubted was that Allie shared the same concern about Ricky that I did. She might find the truth, but I knew for a fact that she'd happily make headline road-kill out of my friend with it.

"So you're really not going to help me?" I asked.

He shook his head. "I wish I could, Maddie."

As much as I hated his stonewalling, the soft look in his eyes almost had me believing he did.

"Fine," I said, then turned on heel and stalked to the elevator again. I glanced back at him over my shoulder as I hit the down button. He was on the phone again, back turned to me, not looking the least bit guilty at letting Ricky hang out to dry.

"Hey."

I spun to my right and came face to face with a woman in a black leather skirt, black tights, black combat boots, and a hot pink baby-doll T-shirt with a silkscreened image of Donald Duck on it. Her eyes were lined in dark make-up, and her hair was darkened with purple tips.

Tina Bender.

"Hey," I returned the greeting.

"I overheard you and Felix," she said, nodding toward the glass walled office. "Bummer."

I nodded. "Yeah, I can't imagine why he's suddenly so hot on journalistic integrity."

Tina shook her head. "Oh, he's not. He's just afraid of scaring off Allie's source." She paused. "However if Allie's source were to get scared off, it would certainly make it harder for *her* to print the story before *I* did."

I raised an eyebrow her way. "What are you proposing, Bender?"

"The interview with Ricky that you promised Allie?"

"I said I'd *try* to get her an interview," I clarified.

But Tina waved me off. "Whatever. Look, I want one, too. If I give you Allie's source, you hook me up with Ricky. Deal?"

I blinked. "Wait - you know who her source is?"

Tina grinned. "I make it my policy to hack Allie's cell whenever she hits the ladies' room. I get some of my best leads that way."

My turn to grin. "Okay, deal. I'll talk to Ricky about an interview." I cringed, wondering if we'd still be friends after I told him he owed interviews to *two* tabloid reporters now. "So spill it. Who's the press leak?"

Tina handed me a Post-It with a phone number written on it. "This number showed up in Allie's call log right before she posted the news of Irina's death, and it showed up again yesterday right before I overheard her telling Felix she had big news to share about Irina."

I raised an eyebrow her way. "You 'overhear' a lot."

She shrugged. "Eavesdropping is a gossip columnist's best skill. Anyway, I'd bet money that number belongs to whoever is feeding Allie stories."

"Bender!" Felix called from his office door.

We both spun around to find him frowning our way.

"Yeah, boss?" she asked, innocently.

"You got that column on Miley's new hair color done yet?"

"On your desk in five," she promised, heading back to her cube.

I shoved the Post-It into my purse and quickly stepped into the elevators, ignoring the blue-eyed stare I could feel searing into my back from Felix's glass-walled office.

The doors shut, the elevator spit me back out on the ground floor, and as soon as I hit the parking lot I pulled the Post-It out again, dialing on my cell.

Four rings in, it was answered with a familiar, "'Sup bitches?"

Bingo. I had my leak.

CHAPTER ELEVEN

———

Two freeways later, we were camped out on the *Dancing with Celebrities* set, which looked surprisingly like it had the first day that Dana and I had arrived to watch Ricky practice. Clearly they were following Hollywood's number one motto: the show must go on. Grips and PA's scattered around the warehouse, pulling cables, setting lights, shouting to one another from across the cavernous room. Director types sat behind monitors, lining up shots, and dancers twirled, lifted, and stretched in every corner. The only noticeable difference was that instead of the spotlight being trained on Ricky and Irina, it was now trained on Kaylie, her multi-colored hair swishing around her face as her partner, Sven, twirled her in a wild swing number.

I had to admit as I watched her glide across the dance floor, she actually had a good chance of taking the title now that Irina and Ricky were out of the running. She was cute, looked good in the little sequined numbers, and actually had some rhythm.

And I suspected had Allie on speed dial as well.

The music ended, and Sven finished off their routine with a lift that had him grunting and Kaylie soaring above his head. He dropped her back down on the ground, mumbled a few notes to her about her footwork, then the director yelled that they were taking five and resetting to rehearse again.

I took that as my cue to move.

"Kaylie," I called, pushing toward her with the twins in Gargantu-stroller as quickly as we could navigate the narrow walkways between the stages.

Kaylie spun around, recognition taking a moment to dawn in her eyes as she watched us approach. "Oh. Hey. The GF and the BFF," she said, nodding to both Dana and me.

"Right. We have a few questions for you."

"Yeah, well, I'm kinda, like, busy now. We're totally behind with rehearsals," she said, pointing to the stage she'd just vacated. "You know. What with the death and all," she added, making it sound about as inconvenient as slow traffic on the 101.

"That's what we wanted to talk to you about," I told her.

"Me? Why? I don't know anything about it."

"You certainly know enough to give Allie Quick an earful," Dana jumped in.

I watched Kaylie's reaction carefully. Her over-plucked brows pulled together. "Who?"

"Don't bother playing dumb blonde with us," Dana told her. "We're dumb blonde experts."

Hmm. I wasn't sure that totally came out the right way.

"What she means is, we know you've been funneling information to Allie at the *Informer*," I added.

Kaylie bit her lip, crimson lipstick flaking off onto her teeth. "Nuh-uh," she said, though it was a weak protest.

"I think you have," I pressed. "I think you told her about the wardrobe pieces going missing, about Irina's murder, and about the argument between Irina and her sister."

Kaylie looked left then right, as if for an escape route. But with Gargantu-stroller pinning her in, there was none. Max let out a cry from his seat, as if to hammer home the point.

"Okay, fine," Kaylie said, lowering her voice. "I might have called the *Informer* once or twice."

"Ha!" Dana cried in triumph.

"Shh," Kaylie said, putting a finger to her lips. "Look, no one can know, okay?" She glanced around the crowded soundstage, quickly pointing us in the direction of her dressing room. "I signed a non-disclosure before coming on the show. Anyone finds out I've been ratting, they're gonna pull my contract."

"So why risk it?" I asked, following her into the privacy of her dressing room. As soon as I navigated the stroller in, she shut the door behind us.

"I needed the cash. I'm almost twenty," she said.

"And?" Dana asked.

"And I'm not a *Teen* Mom anymore. They're dropping me from the show after this season."

"And Allie offered you cash for information," I added.

Kaylie nodded. "It was an offer I couldn't refuse. I mean, you know how much that pink house set me back? My new Mercedes? Dude, just my pool alone is like way crazy to maintain. I never knew being rich was, like, so expensive."

Oh, brother. I resisted the urge to roll my eyes.

"Did you just roll your eyes at me?" Kaylie asked.

Okay, I almost resisted.

"What exactly did you tell Allie?" I asked.

"Well," she said, biting her lipstick off again. "At first I just told her that wardrobe was being stolen."

"But then Irina was killed."

Kaylie nodded again. "Right. Totally way more interesting than a few missing clothes, right? At least, I thought it might be to Allie."

"And then you told her about seeing Irina argue with her twin sister."

Kaylie nodded again. "I didn't think anything of it at the time. I mean, Irina argued with everyone, so I didn't think it that weird that she'd argue with a sister, too, right?"

"Until she died," Dana added.

"Right, until then. Which got me thinking,"

"That maybe the sister killed her?" I suggested.

Kaylie shook her head. "That maybe I could capitalize on anything I'd ever seen Irina do. Holy cow, you know how much Allie was paying me for each little detail about Irina's last movements I sent her? Like, tons. I figured I'd milk that Allie chick for all she was worth."

Suddenly, I almost felt sorry for Allie. "Okay, so tell us about the sister. Katrina," I prompted.

"Well, it was last week. Just before the last show aired. I walked past Irina's dressing room, and the door was open just a little. I heard Irina's voice first. She was yelling in Russian about something. Kinda par for the course with Irina."

"And then?"

"Well, then I heard a second voice. So naturally I was curious."

"Naturally."

"Anyway, I kinda peeked in and saw this woman who was, like, Irina's total mirror image. I figured it had to be her sister. I mean, they were like twins or something."

"What exactly did she look like?" Dana asked.

Kaylie blinked at her. "I just told you. She looked like Irina."

"What was she wearing?" I probed.

Kaylie scrunched up her face. "Tight stuff. Leopard print. Looked kinda cheap to me."

I raised an eyebrow. If it looked cheap to Kaylie, it had to be darn near free.

"What else? Hair color? Eye color? Anything?"

Kaylie shrugged. "Like I said, she just looked like Irina."

"What did you hear them say?" I asked.

"Sorry. It was all in Russian. I caught the sister's name, but that was it."

"Can you remember anything they said? Anything at all?" Dana pleaded, desperation lacing her voice.

Kaylie did more lipstick eating. "They did keep saying one word over and over." She paused, eyes staring off into space as she recalled it. "Zing-ya."

"What does that mean?"

She shrugged again. "Beats me."

"Anything else you can tell us?"

"Sorry. That's all I know. For reals." She paused. "Look, you won't tell the producers about this, will you?"

I shook my head. "On one condition?"

"Anything," she promised.

"Call me before you call Allie next time."

*   *   *

Kaylie skittered back to the sound stage to reset for another rehearsal just as Max started to yell again in his seat. I picked him up, jiggling him while Dana fished out her cell and pulled up a Russian-to-English translation page. She typed in the word "Zing-ya". Nothing. She tried a slightly different spelling. Still nada. After several tries, and several bytes into her data plan, she finally found a site where the phonetic version of the word transformed into the print word: деньги. Which, after plugging that into a translation page, she found out translated into the word "money".

"So Irina and her sister were arguing about money," Dana mused, looking down at the readout.

I nodded. "And depending on how much 'zing-ya' they were talking about, it might make for reasonable motive for murder."

"We need to find that sister," Dana said.

We both looked down the hallway toward Irina's dressing room.

While yellow crime scene tape still sealed Ricky's door shut, Irina's was free of barricades. I looked over both shoulders. A couple of wardrobe people were hanging out in a doorway three down, and a PA was running through the hall with a clipboard in hand. None paid any attention to us. I slowly made my way down the hall to Irina's door, trying to look like I had every right to be there. I grabbed the door handle and gingerly turned. It twisted in my hand, and the door easily popped open.

If that wasn't an invitation to snoop, I didn't know what was.

With one more quick over-the-shoulder, I pushed forward, and Dana and I slipped into the room, Gargantu-stroller and all.

I jiggled Max up and down, praying he stayed silent in my arms as I quickly surveyed the room. A vanity sat on one side, flanked by lights. On the other was a wardrobe rack, filled with a dozen glittery dresses and a couple pairs of street clothes. Empty coffee cups sat on a table near the wall, along with make-up, hair pins, and various other personal items. It looked like no one had cleaned out the room since Irina had been here.

Lucky for us.

"What are we looking for?" Dana whispered, as I started opening drawers in the vanity.

I shrugged. "I don't know. Anything that could lead us to the sister."

Dana nodded, opening a closet and finding more costumes and several pairs of shoes.

I scooped up the contents of Irina's wastebasket, coming up with receipts for lunch, a couple of cocktail napkins, and several used tissues full of stage make-up. I looked through the cosmetics in a bag on the vanity, finding nothing more incriminating than the fact that Irina bought supermarket brand eyeliner. I moved to the wardrobe rack, finding custom garments that had me drooling and dying to try them on. But nothing that screamed sister or secret killer.

"Man, she had a lot of dancing shoes," Dana said, gesturing to the line of footwear in the closet.

I paused, checking them out. She was right. Several ballroom dancing shoes in colors ranging from hot pink to nude to jet black lined the closet floor. Most of them were soft, supple, and made for movement. The heels were three inches or lower, flat across the back.

Most of them.

One pair of leopard print platforms near the back of the closet was decidedly not dancing shoes.

I kneeled down and picked them up.

Dana raised an eyebrow. "Leopard? Seriously? God, what a slut." She paused. "Is it wrong to call the dead a slut?"

I shook my head. "Not if she was sleeping with your boyfriend."

"Thanks." She paused. "I think."

"But these aren't Irina's shoes," I pointed out.

Dana cocked her head at me. "Okay, I give. How do you know that?"

"Look at the other ones."

Dana did. Then she looked back at the ones in my hands. Then back to the row in the closet. Finally I saw the light bulb go off behind her eyes. "They're the wrong size!"

I nodded. "They're close, but these are eights, and I'd bet those are nines."

Dana picked up a pair of nude dancing shoes and checked the inside tag. She nodded. "You're right. Nine, wide." She paused. "Is it wrong of me to be glad she had fat feet?"

I shook my head. "There's no way a nine wide would fit in this eight."

Dana took the other leopard shoe in her hand. "So, you think these belong to her sister?" she asked.

I shrugged. "Well, they're not Irina's, and it didn't sound like she was close enough with anyone on set that she'd be sharing closet space."

"So the sister is the slut," Dana said, scrunching her nose up at the platform. "I guess it runs in the family."

I turned the shoe over. On the bottom of the shoe, someone had written in black sharpie. "Property of Glitter Kat." I raised an eyebrow showing the bottom to Dana.

"Glitter Kat," she read. "You think that's Katrina?"

"It has to be." I paused, remembering what I'd seen on one of the cocktail napkins in the wastebasket. "And I think I know where to find her."

I ran to the trash and dug around, coming out with the napkin that had caught my eye. I smoothed it on the table. The logo on the corner read, "Glitter Galaxy" with an address in Industry. Right next to a silhouette of a naked woman hanging off a pole.

Dana gasped over my shoulder. "Oh. Em. Gee. It's a strip club!"

I nodded. "It looks like dancing ran in the Sokolov family."

CHAPTER TWELVE

——

The City of Industry is one giant block of warehouses after another, housing the inventory for most of Los Angeles's import and export businesses. At least half of which are legal. A warehouse full of toys from China might be right next to a warehouse full of overpriced Scandinavian furniture, next to a warehouse full of Coach knock-offs. Between the warehouses are nestled trucking companies, cheap Chinese buffets, and gentlemen's clubs where no actual gentlemen would step foot.

The Glitter Galaxy was a one-story, square building sitting between a John Deere wholesaler and a warehouse with the name "China-Co" printed on the side. The parking lot was surprisingly full for a Tuesday afternoon, sprinkled with a mix of pick-up trucks, sedans, and big rigs. We were the only minivan.

I parked in a slot off to the side and stepped out into the glare of the Galaxy's neon signage. Clinging to their roof was a nude woman with huge neon yellow nipples. I looked down at Livvie and Max in their car seats.

"You know, I'm not having a real 'good mom' moment right now," I told Dana.

She paused, looked down at the babies, up at the neon lady. "Well... let's look at it this way: You did breastfeed them, right?"

I nodded.

"Then it's not like they'll see anything in there that they haven't seen before."

"That almost made me feel better."

"Don't worry. I'm pretty sure they're too young to be scarred for life. I think you have to be at least six months old for that."

I hoped she was right as I grabbed two kangaroo pouch carriers, popped a baby in each one, then handed a carrier to Dana.

"Oh, actually..." Dana said, holding Max by the armpits as the pouch dangled around him. "Do you mind if I wear Livvie?"

I shrugged. "Sure. I didn't realize you had a preference."

"Oh, no, not a baby preference," she clarified, swapping tots with me and strapping Livvie onto her chest. "It's just that Livvie's carrier is powder pink, and it matches better with the canary yellow in my sweats, don't you think?"

I was about to roll my eyes at her, but as I looked over, I had to admit, she was right. Hey, if you gotta wear a baby, you might as well accessorize them well. Plus, I was glad she was taking more interest in her looks. Even if it was just accessorizing her sweats.

I strapped Max to my own chest, his baby blue carrier actually going very well with the red top and white, denim pants I'd selected that morning. Then I beeped the car locked and pushed through the doors to the Glitter Galaxy.

The interior was dark, windowless, and smelled like stale cigarettes despite the statewide ban. A long, cat-walk style stage took up most of the floor space, jutting into the center of the room. It was painted green and doused with a healthy sprinkling of glitter, like a child's art project gone awry. Groupings of tables and chairs sat near it, half of them full of droopy-eyed guys with their hands under the tables as they watched the action on the stage. Around the perimeter of the room were plastic booths, painted white with red trim to look like space ships.

A sign above the stage proclaimed in neon that we had entered the "Glitter Galaxy", and an advertisement in hand written paper next to that said that drinks were half priced to all earthlings from 3-6pm on Thursdays.

On the stage was a woman in a space helmet, wearing tall platform heels and nothing else, wiggled her naked butt to Elton John's "Rocket Man" being pumped through the speakers.

Instinctively I covered Max's eyes.

A woman with long dark hair and almond eyes approached us. She stood at least a head shorter than me and wore a lime green bikini with little aliens painted on it. She looked down at the babies strapped to our chests. "Eighteen and over only here," she said in a thick, Asian accent.

"I promise they won't watch," I said, still covering Max's eyes.

She raised an eyebrow at me. "Hey, we're pretty open here, but we got to draw the line somewhere."

"Look, we're not here to..." I trailed off, thinking of those hands under the tables. "We're here to see Katrina," I settled on. "Glitter Kat."

The woman paused. "You know Kat?"

"We know her sister. Or, knew," I corrected myself.

She stuck a hand out my way. "Ling."

"Maddie." I shook, trying to block out where that hand might have been. "Is Kat here?"

Ling shook her head, a frown settling between her delicate brows. "She hasn't been in all week. I was actually starting to worry about her. It wasn't like her not to show for Thursday."

"Why do you say that?" I asked.

"It's our big money night," she said, pointing to the half-priced drinks sign. "Not that I'm complaining. I took her slot. Made three large. Nice night."

"Three hundred?" I asked, impressed.

"Thousand."

I blinked at her. "You're kidding."

"No way, José," she said, her thick accent stumbling over the Americanism. "I don't kid about green."

I did a little mental math, trying to calculate how many pairs of new boots that was.

"When was the last time you saw Kat?" Dana asked.

Ling scrunched up her face, her eyes searching the ceiling for answers. "Monday night."

The day before Irina was killed. An interesting coincidence.

"Did you ever meet Kat's sister?" I asked.

Ling shook her head. "No. But this isn't really the kind of place you invite your family, you know what I mean?" She paused, looking down at the baby I was wearing. "Well, *most* people don't."

"Did she ever talk about her sister?" I asked, ignoring the jab at my parenting. Hey, I still had Max's eyes covered. "Her name was Irina."

Ling narrowed her eyes at me. "*Was*? Something happen to her?"

"She's dead," Dana said.

Ling clucked her tongue. "Oh, that sucks."

"Katrina never mentioned her?" I asked.

She shook her head again. "Sorry. I never heard her talk about a sister. But Kat wasn't really that easy to get close to."

"How so?"

Ling scrunched her nose up again. "She had a terrible temper. Always yelling. She even yelled at her uncle when he was here."

I perked up. "Uncle?"

"Yeah. This Russian guy. He comes in last week and says he's looking for Kat. That he's her uncle."

"And Kat yelled at him?"

She nodded. "She got all upset when she saw him. Then they went outside, and I heard them arguing in the parking lot."

"What did they say?"

She shook her head. "I don't know. It was all in Russian."

"Can you describe this uncle?" Dana asked.

"Tall, dark hair, pale skin. Kinda good looking in a Euro-trash way. Mindy was even gonna ask him out," she said, gesturing to the space girl on the stage. "But I told her not to bother."

"Why is that?" I asked.

"He was wearing an earring. It was a big, diamond stud. In his right ear. You know what that means." She winked at me. "Fruity."

"Wait - I thought left ear meant gay," Dana put in.

"That's what Mindy, thought, too. We argued about it all afternoon after he left."

"Anything else you can tell us about him?" I asked.

She shrugged her slim shoulders. "Sorry. I didn't pay much attention. He argued with Kat, then he left, and Kat did her set. I figured it was no biggie, right?"

"Ling!" a guy shouted from the last booth.

"What?" she yelled back over the music.

"You're up!"

"Sorry. Gotta go shake my money maker," she told us, heading off toward a silver, beaded curtain to the right of the stage.

I watched her, digesting what she'd told us. "So our mystery guy visited both Irina and Katrina," I mused out loud.

Dana nodded. "And he argued with both."

"And then Katrina argues with Irina about money, and Irina ends up dead."

"And Katrina takes off," Dana added. "Totally suspicious."

"Totally," I agreed. "What do you want to bet the Russian guy wasn't really Kat's uncle?"

"About as much as I'd want to bet that Kat had something to do with her sister's death." She paused. "Maybe Irina wanted money from her to buy votes?" Her eyes lit up. "Maybe she hired the Russian guy to shake her sister down for cash."

I shot her a look. "'Shake her down'? You really have been watching too many Scorsese movies."

"Or maybe Irina was blackmailing her sister for money," Dana went on, undeterred. "Maybe she knew a secret about her from back home in Russia. Maybe, they were, like, international criminals on the run!"

I opened my mouth to tell her I was officially cutting her off from HBO when my cell buzzed to life.

"Hello?" I answered before I checked the readout. I know, rookie mistake. One I regretted as soon as I heard the familiar voice on the other end.

"Hey, babe."

Ramirez.

"Uh, hi. Honey."

"What?" he yelled.

"I said 'hi.'"

"I can hardly hear you," he responded. "Where are you?"

"Uh..." I looked at the stage where Space Girl was scooping up the last of her twenties, stuffing them into the top of her boots. "Nowhere."

"The music is really loud. Can you turn it down?"

"Uh, not really. I'm..."

I looked to Dana for help.

"Shopping," she supplied.

"I'm shopping." I cringed at the lie.

"God, where are you shopping?"

"Hot Topic," I lied. "Teenagers like loud music." I felt guilt spreading through me like a rash and tried to block it out as I asked, "So, what's up?"

"Got a break. I'm heading home for lunch. I thought maybe I'd get some twin time in."

Oh snap. I totally forgot about lunch. "Uh, right. Sure. Great," I said, gesturing wildly to Dana that we had to exit, pronto. She nodded, catching my drift and leading the way back toward the front doors.

"Cool. You're, what, fifteen minutes away?"

I closed my eyes, thinking a really dirty word. Hot Topic at the mall was fifteen minutes away. I, on the other hand, was a good half hour. "Something like that," I hedged.

"Okay, meet you at home then."

"Greatloveyouseeyousoon," I slurred together double time as I hung up and jumped into the min-van. We had the babies strapped into seats in record time. I pulled out of the parking lot, praying the green light gods were with me. If not, I was going to have to make a big sacrifice to the kissing-up-to-your-husband gods later.

Only running two orange lights, I made it home in twenty-two minutes.

Unfortunately, Ramirez had made it home in fewer, as his SUV was already parked in the driveway.

I tried to calm my pulse back to normal as I shooed Dana back to her own car, grabbed a twin in each arm, and walked through the front door.

"Hey," Ramirez said, coming out of the back bedroom. He leaned down to kiss the head of each baby.

"Hey yourself," I said, only slightly out of breath.

"The little guys give you any trouble?" he asked, taking Livvie from me.

I shook my head. "Nope, they were little angels!"

"What did you get?"

"Huh?"

Ramirez frowned at me as he headed to the refrigerator. "You said you were shopping. What did you get?"

"Oh. Right." I looked down at my hands, sans shopping bags. "Uh, we were more window shopping than anything."

"Oh," he said from the kitchen. "Cool." He opened the refrigerator, pulling out a loaf of bread and some mustard.

I prayed that was him dropping the subject. Shoving guilt down, I set Max in his swing and followed Ramirez into the kitchen.

"So, you got a break today, huh?" I asked, leaning my elbows on the counter in front of him.

He nodded. "Yeah, we got a potential lead in the case coming in, but it won't be ready until late this afternoon. Thought I'd take advantage of the time and spend it with my lovely family," he said, planting a fly-by kiss on my cheek as he reached for the salami from the refrigerator behind me.

"A lead?" I asked, perking up.

"Uh-huh." He squirted mustard onto a slice of sourdough, reaching into the drawer for a knife to spread it.

I waited. "Well?"

"Well what?"

"Well, don't leave me hanging. What's the lead?"

His eyes twinkled with a devilish gleam that said leaving me hanging was exactly what he'd intended to do. "Oh. You want to know what it is?"

I swatted him on the arm with a napkin. "You're killing me here," I said, taking Livvie back from him so he could cut his sandwich.

"Well, since you've been so cool about being left out of the loop on this one-"

Ouch. Guilt washed over me heavier than a storm.

"-forensics came back with analysis of contaminants left at the scene."

"Contaminants?"

"Hair mostly."

"Oh. And?"

"And there were a few contributors. The victim. Ricky."

I cringed. "But his hair should be in his dressing room, right?"

Ramirez nodded. "True. Howeeeeeever," he said, drawing the word out.

"Yes?"

He grinned down at me. He was enjoying this way too much. I felt some of that guilt slipping away. "There was another contributor."

"The killer?"

"It's possible."

"Whose is it?"

"Unknown contributor at the moment. They're running a DNA profile now, but we'll need something to compare it to before we have anything conclusive."

I pursed my lips, jiggling Livvie in my arms. What did you want to bet that Unknown Contributor was our Russian with a thing for diamonds?

CHAPTER THIRTEEN

———

Two salami sandwiches and a round of "Itsy Bitsy Spider" later, Ramirez headed back to the precinct, and I headed to the nursery to put the twins down for a nap. As soon as the silence descended, I grabbed my cell and hit number three on my speed dial.

"Maddie, dahling, how are you?" Marco answered.

"Fab. Listen, right ear or left ear? Which one do gay guys wear studs in?"

"Oh, honey. No one wears studs anymore. That was so 2000's."

I rolled my eyes. "Humor me. Assume a guy is very fashion stunted. Which ear would indicate that he's also into guys?"

"Right."

"You sure?"

"Definitely. But you can borrow my gaydar if you're iffy on someone."

I pursed my lips together. "Actually, I'm trying to find someone, and I don't have much to go on. Just an earring."

"Describe him to me," Marco demanded.

While expecting Marco to know every gay man in L.A. was a little like expecting Joan Rivers to know *every* plastic surgeon in Beverly Hills, I figured it was worth a shot. I gave him the brief description we'd gotten.

"Doesn't ring a bell. Sorry."

"I figured as much."

"But I'll ask around and see if anyone knows him," Marco offered.

"Fair enough," I agreed. "Thanks, Marco."

I hung up and settled on the couch with a DVR-ed episode of *Dancing with Celebrities*. I watched Irina's last performance, dancing the mambo with Ricky. I had to admit, she was graceful, smooth, beautiful. I wondered what her sister had been like. How had their lives been so different that Irina had ended up on TV and Katrina at the Glitter Galaxy? While I watched, I grabbed my laptop and googled everything I could about Irina.

Her official bio was slim, which wasn't totally surprising as this was her first season on DWC. She'd come from Russia four years earlier. She'd been a back-up dancer in a few music videos, then landed the DWC gig. No mention of her life prior to arriving in the U.S. No mention of a mysterious Russian guy.

My cell buzzed to life beside me, Marco's name lighting the display.

I quickly answered. "Hey."

"I found your Russian," Marco sing-songed into my ear.

I sat bolt upright. "No way!" What do you know? Turns out maybe Marco did know every gay man in town.

"Way. Turns out a friend of a friend of a friend saw him at a club the other night."

"You're sure it's the same guy?"

"New in town, Russian accent, diamond stud in one ear."

"So far so good. What's his name?"

"My friend's friend's friend didn't get a name."

"Crap."

"Turns out the Russian was more into the anonymity thing. But, he did take my friend's friend's friend home with him."

I felt my hope perking up again. "And home is?"

"A hotel. The Bayshore Inn in NoHo."

"Marco, you are an absolute gem!" I squealed.

"I know. I am, right?" he agreed.

I hung up and quickly texted Dana saying we had a lead.

Then I texted my mom. As much as I was dying to follow up on our mystery man, the last place I wanted to drag my precious babies was a seedy motel in North Hollywood. Especially since I'd already dragged them to a seedy strip joint in Industry.

Luckily, Mom was free and said she'd be there to babysit in twenty minutes.

Unluckily, the twins woke up from their naps in ten and had worked themselves into the foulest mood on the planet by the time Dana arrived. Their cries had reached decibel levels that even Spinal Tap couldn't achieve.

"Sorry, they're in a mood this afternoon," I yelled to Dana as she came into the living room.

"Great," she yelled back. "Please tell me we're not taking them with us?"

I shook my head. "No. Reinforcements are on the way. My mom is coming to watch them for a couple of hours."

"Thank God."

"What?" I asked, leaning in.

"I said, 'Thank God.' Geeze, are they okay?" Dana asked.

I picked Max up, patting his back. Were they okay? I wondered. Had I been leaving them with sitters too much? Did they realize I was leaving again? I bit my lip, guilt hitting me. The sensation was starting to become my constant companion.

I didn't have much time to contemplate it though as the doorbell rang, followed by a head popping in the door.

"Hello?" Mom said. "Anyone home?"

"I assume that's a rhetorical question," I answered, shouting over Livvie's cries this time.

"Oh, what's wrong with my babies?" Mom asked, coming into the room cooing. Mrs. Rosenblatt, in a screaming orange muumuu, followed a step behind her. Mom grabbed Livvie from me, patting her on the back. Amazingly, the cries ceased immediately.

An odd sensation fluttered in my stomach.

"How did you do that?" I asked.

Mom blinked at me. "Do what?"

"Make her stop crying?"

She shrugged. "Oh, my grandbabies just know when Grandma's here. Don't you, you wittle, bitty, wovey, dovey," she said, making kissing faces at Livvie.

I felt a frown settle between my eyebrows as Mrs. R picked up Max, and his cries stopped too. He burped, then did a big, delighted smile at her. Great, even the psychic had a better touch than I did.

"Thanks for coming to watch the twins," I told mom, trying not to take their sudden angelic behavior personally. "I know I've been asking you to babysit a lot lately."

Mom waved me off. "Don't worry a bit about it. I'm tied to my phone this afternoon anyway."

I raised an eyebrow her way. "Do I want to know why?"

"A hot auction," Mrs. R explained. "She's got the eBay app on there."

I thunked the palm of my hand on my forehead. "Mom, you are dangerous with that phone."

She frowned at me. "That's what Ralph says, too. But," she said, pulling the item in question from her purse, "he'll be changing his tune when he sees what I got him for our anniversary."

I almost hated to asked but… "What did you get him?"

"An Armani blazer. Only worn twice!"

Poor Faux Dad.

* * *

Leaving the babies in Mom's very capable hands, and Mom in the questionable clutches of her online shopping habit, Dana and I got into my minivan and hopped onto the 101.

The city of North Hollywood is known for three things: discount electronics of dubious origin, AA meetings on every other block, and porn studios that number in the hundreds. Usually Magnolia was as far north as I traveled along Laurel Canyon, and as we passed a homeless guy with a shopping cart full of stray cats, I remembered why.

The Bayshore Inn was located a few blocks north of Chandler, in the neighborhood known as "Little Tijuana." Their sign was faded, the paint on the side of the building peeling, and the landscaping limited to a lone cactus propped up against the door to the front office. We parked next to a rusted iron gate that circled a big cement hole in the ground which might have been a pool at one point but was now playing host to a couple of kids in skinny jeans and beanies on skateboards. The guest rooms were all on one main level, circling the pool. I counted twenty from where we stood.

"So, which one do you think our Russian is in?" I asked.

Dana shrugged. "Let's go ask," she suggested, gesturing to the motel office.

"You really think he'll just tell us?" I said, trailing along behind her.

"Trust me, I can get it out of him," she assured me, fluffing her boobs up in her T-shirt.

I followed her into the main office, which smelled like stale burritos and cigars. Behind the counter sat a guy with long, stringy blonde hair, a week's worth of beard, and tattoo sleeves down both arms. He looked up as we walked in and did a long once over on each of us.

"Can I help you?" he asked.

Dana shot him her biggest, brightest, movie star smile and leaned her elbows on the counter. "Gosh, I sure hope so," she said, her voice dripping with enough sugar to attract flies.

"Need a room?" he asked.

"Maybe," Dana said coyly. "But we wanted to ask you a few questions first."

He leaned back in his chair, crossing his arms over his chest. "You do, huh?"

"We were wondering if you could tell us about a guest," I jumped in.

The guy shook his head. "Our guests like to stay private, you know?"

"Oh, I know," Dana said, leaning farther forward so her boobs peeked out the top of her V-neck T. "But if you could do just this one little favor for us, we'd *so* appreciate it." She punctuated the last bit by licking her lips and giving him a seductive stare, full of all kinds of unspoken promises.

The guy shook his head. He looked from Dana's girls to me. "Is she for real?"

Dana frowned. "Yes, I'm for real."

"Look, *chica*, you're in day-old sweats, and I can smell you from here."

Dana gasped, doing an armpit sniff. "You can't!"

The guy did a lopsided smile. "You gonna try to seduce info out of me, you gonna have to do a lot better than..." He paused, waving toward Dana. "...this."

She narrowed her eyes. "I'll have you know I had my hair hot-oiled for forty minutes yesterday. It's silky smooth."

The guy turned to me. "What do you girls really want?"

"We need info on a Russian guy staying here."

"We got lots of guys staying here. I don't pay attention to particulars."

"He wears a diamond earring. And has a thick accent," I added.

"Sorry. Not ringing any bells."

I grabbed my wallet out of my purse and threw a twenty down on the counter. "Remember yet?"

He rolled his eyes.

I added another twenty. "Now?"

He shrugged. "I'm getting closer."

I sighed, draining my shoe fund for the month as I added another twenty. "That's all I have. Take it or leave it."

His hand reached out and took it, shoving my cash into the back pocket of his jeans. "Fine. Your Russian guy is in room twelve. But I haven't seen him all day."

"Thanks!" I called, already leaving the office.

Dana sulked behind me. "That's it, I'm losing my touch. You know, between two-thousand-one and two-thousand-eleven I didn't get a single parking ticket. I used to be able to seduce my way out of anything. Now I can't even get a sleazy motel manager's attention."

"Relax," I told her. "His lack of interest had more to do with your outfit than a lack-of-touch."

She paused. "Are the sweats really that bad?"

"Yes."

"Geeze, you didn't have to answer so quickly."

"It's time for tough love."

"Fine, I'll go home and change after this," she mumbled.

"Shh," I said, approaching a door with the number twelve affixed in rusted numbers.

She shushed, following me as we both listened for any sound from the other side. Nothing.

"Maybe Sleazy Guy's right. Maybe he's out," Dana whispered.

"Maybe he's sleeping," I said, trying to peek between the curtains in the windows. No such luck. They were cheap, but they were private.

"Maybe we should just wait for him to come back," I said.

But before I could turn back to the car, Dana shot her hand out and tried the door knob. It turned easily in her hand, the door popping open.

We both looked at each other. Anyone who left their doors unlocked in this neighborhood was either stupid or such a bad-ass they were welcoming a fight.

I really hoped he had a low IQ.

"Hello?" Dana called, taking a step into the room. I followed a tentative step behind her. "Anyone here?" she asked.

The curtains were pulled and the lights turned off, making it dark despite the sunshine outside. It smelled musty, like it had been shut up for awhile, and a sour scent hung in the air, like food left out too long.

I covered my nose against the cloying odor as I took in the surroundings. A small TV sat on a dresser. The bed had a floral spread in a pattern made to hide stains, and the floor was done in matted brown shag.

"Hello? Russian guy?" Dana called again. Though, in the shoebox sized room it was clear we were alone.

"Let's get out of here," I said, fear prickling the back of my neck. As much as I wanted answers about Irina, I did not want to surprise a potentially lethal guy in a dark room. Somehow the sunshine outside was feeling much safer.

"Okay. But let's just take a quick look around first," Dana said, moving farther into the room instead. "Maybe there's something here with his name on it."

Despite the nagging fear in my throat, I did, opening a dresser drawer as Dana checked the nightstand. I found underwear, socks, a couple pairs of jeans, and a handful of condoms.

"Nothing here," I said. "You?"

Dana shook her head, straightening up. "He's our guy though. He's been to the Glitter Galaxy," she said, holding up a stained cocktail napkin bearing the familiar logo.

"Good. Let's go ask about him there some more," I said, suddenly preferring the bright, loud atmosphere of the strip club to the too-quiet sensation in the dark room.

"Lemme just check the bathroom," Dana protested, going to a door to the right of the closet. "Maybe he has a prescription with his name on it or something that he…" she trailed off, going stiff in the doorway.

That fear prickle kicked into overdrive. "What?" I asked, coming up behind her.

Though she didn't have to answer as I peeked over her shoulder and saw for myself.

Lying on the bathroom floor, legs twisted underneath him, was a dark haired guy with one sparkling diamond stud in his right ear.

And one wet, red bullet hole in his chest.

CHAPTER FOURTEEN

———

I blinked, listening to the sound of my own heart beating like a jackhammer in my chest, Dana gasping, and someone screaming at the top of her lungs. It took me a minute to realize the screamer was me. When I finally paused for air, I grabbed Dana by the arm.

"We gotta get out of here."

She nodded dumbly, still making little gasping sounds, as we turned and sprinted to my car. We jumped into the nice, safe minivan, locked the doors, and put our seatbelts on just for good measure. I stared out the windshield at the now ajar door to room twelve.

"Ohmigod, he was dead," Dana said, stating the obvious.

My turn to nod dumbly.

"Like, shot dead."

I nodded again.

"You think we should call the police?"

I shook my head violently from side to side. "Ramirez will kill me. Let them do it."

Our screams had already alerted several of the other motel guests. Two guys in leather pants emerged from room twenty, a woman in platforms and spandex from room ten, and from the room next door to our dead guy, a Hispanic man in a cowboy hat. Chances were that in a matter of minutes, the police would already be here. And any way that brought the police and didn't involve Maddie being the body-finder was a road to marital bliss.

"Come on, let's go before the press arrive," Dana said, her mind going in the same direction as mine. Only her nemesis was a perky blonde reporter.

I rolled the engine over and peeled out of the parking lot, making a sharp left onto Tujunga. It wasn't until we hit the freeway that my hands stopped shaking.

"I need a milkshake," I declared to the world at large.

Dana spun on me. "Maddie! You're on a diet!"

"Dana, I just found a dead body. If I don't get some kind of comfort food into my system soon, I may go into shock."

She bit her lip. But she must have seen the irrefutable logic in my statement as she said, "There's a Foster's Freeze on Glenoaks Boulevard. Make a right."

I did. Ignoring the obvious fact that my friend's junk food addiction had gone into overdrive if she knew where the nearest Foster's was.

Two chocolate milkshakes with extra whipped cream and cherries later, I was starting to feel human.

That is, until my cell buzzed in my purse. I picked it up, checking the readout. Ramirez.

Was I bad person that I let it go to voicemail?

Instead, I pointed my car toward home. After the sight I'd seen, I needed to see my babies, to hold chubby little feet in my hands.

As soon as I walked in the door, I immediately felt better, the sight of my familiar home, my happy babies playing on the floor, and my mommy (yes, in a crisis she was still "Mommy") soothing some normalcy back into me.

I picked up the nearest baby, snuggling up against his soft, pudgy cheek.

He immediately started crying.

"It's okay, sweets," I said, jiggling him gently up and down. Only he clearly didn't agree with my assessment of the situation, yelling louder. "Come on, Max, it's Mama," I told him.

"Uh, Mads," Mom said. "That's Livvie."

I looked down at the crying baby swathed in neutral yellow. I peeked in the diaper. Sure enough, I had a girl.

"Oh my God, I don't even know my own kids anymore!" I wailed.

"Don't worry," Mom said, taking the baby from me. (Who immediately stopped crying, by the way.)

"I'm a horrible, absent mother!"

"They're just tired," Mrs. Rosenblatt reassured me. "A little nap, and they'll be as good as new."

I hoped she was right as I watched Mom settle both babies into their swings before taking her departure.

Only as soon as the front door shut behind them, the twins started crying again.

It took an hour of bottles, burps, and binkies before they finally calmed down again, content to sit in their carriers and watch *Dora the Explorer* (Okay, it really wasn't that bad of a show.) until they fell asleep.

It wasn't until they were settled in their cribs for the night that I was finally ready to process what we'd found in the motel. I curled up on my bed with a cozy blanket and a pad of sketch paper. At the top I wrote, "Russian with diamond earring NOT murderer". Whatever his connection to the Sokolov girls, clearly, he couldn't very well be our killer if he'd just gotten himself killed.

I tapped my pencil against the paper. So who was?

Irina had been talking about buying votes with our Russian guy. Right after that, she and Katrina had argued about money. Had the money been for the votes? Something else? Ling had mentioned that Kat had a temper. Had it been bad enough to kill both her sister and the Russian guy? And, if so, where was she now?

And then there was the small nagging question of how did Katrina manage to get onto the DWC set the day she'd killed Irina? Granted, she'd visited with her sister the day before, but, as I well knew, unless you were specifically on that day's list, it was no easy task to get in.

So who had been on the list?

I flipped to a new page on my pad and wrote down Kaylie's name. The Teen Mom had already confessed to us that she was ratting on her fellow stars for money. She was desperate for cash, and now that Irina was out of the picture, Kaylie had a good chance of winning the title and the prize money that went with it. Had she been desperate enough to kill Irina over it? It was possible. Though I wasn't sure how the dead Russian guy fit into all of that.

However there was one person who might have had it in for both Irina and the diamond studded guy.

I wrote Shaniqua's name down. Shaniqua had accused Irina of pulling a cheating scheme with the Russian by buying foreign votes. Clearly Shaniqua had been upset over it. But had she really killed over it. Twice?

And then there was Ricky.

I stared at the paper, not quite able to make myself write his name down. Did I honestly think he had it in him to kill someone? No. Not really. But he had no alibi, all the means in the world, and even a possible motive if he'd been sleeping with Irina and didn't want Dana to find out. Though, Ricky would have to be awfully stupid to kill Irina in his own dressing room and then not even come up with an alibi. And the Ricky I knew wasn't Einstein, but he wasn't that dumb.

So, who was?

I chewed the end of my pencil and drew some shoe doodles on the side of my pad of paper. I tapped the eraser on my lips, did some productive staring at the ceiling, but nothing brilliant came to me.

I was just putting the finishing touches on a doodle of a slingback with a studded ankle strap when I heard the front door open.

"That you?" I asked, peeking into the living room to find my husband. I stole a glance at his face, trying to gauge his mood. As in, did he know his wife had fled the scene of a crime that afternoon?

"Yep," came Ramirez's answer. "Sorry I'm late. I tried to call, but your phone went to voicemail."

I glanced up at the clock. I hadn't even realized how much time I'd spent doodling. It was after eight. "No problem," I told him. "I was just going to start dinner. Hungry?"

"Starving. I haven't eaten since lunch," he said, following me into the kitchen.

I bit my lip, hoping that finding a dead Russian in a motel room hadn't been the cause. "Rough afternoon?" I asked tentatively.

He nodded, pulling a beer from the fridge and cracking open the top. "Very." He paused, taking a long drag. "How was your afternoon? The kids give you any trouble?"

"Nope!" Mostly because they were with my Mom, but I didn't feel compelled to add that. "You make any headway on Irina's case?" I asked, steering the conversation away from my exploits.

But Ramirez shook his head. "No, I got called out on something else."

"Oh? Anything interesting?"

"Not really. Shooting at a motel in North Hollywood."

I froze. "Oh," I squeaked out. "Who?"

"Some Russian guy."

I turned away, sure my face had guilt written all over it.

"The police have any leads on the shooter?" I managed to ask, opening the freezer and studying the contents to avoid eye contact.

"Several witnesses saw a couple of women leaving the scene."

I closed my eyes, and felt my knees go weak. "They did?" I squeaked out.

"Yeah, but no one was close enough to get a description. Besides, the witnesses weren't real reliable. Couple of junkies and a prostitute."

I did a sigh of relief.

"You okay?"

I spun around. "Sure, yes, great. Why?"

He shrugged, taking another sip of his beer. "You just sounded funny, that's all."

"Nope. I'm fine and dandy. Great. Fabulous."

"Hmph," he grunted.

I cleared my throat. "Chicken or fish?" I asked, coming out of the freezer with two frozen meals as a clear distraction technique.

He paused, his eyes roving my face. And for a split second I thought he knew everything from my babysitter reliance to my body finding.

I did my best poker face, holding the frozen offerings in front of me.

But it must have just been my overactive guilty conscience, because a second later it passed, and he said, "Chicken."

I quickly pulled the entrée from the package and popped it into the microwave, keeping my back to him. My poker face could only last so long.

"You know, you're going to have to make this up to me sometime," he said.

I sucked in a breath and spun around. "What do you mean?"

"All the frozen meals. I know you're on a diet, but why do I have to suffer?" he asked, the hint of a smile in his voice.

I did a mental sigh of relief. "Tell you what," I said. "How about you learn to cook, and you can make it up to yourself?"

"I can cook," he protested.

I raised an eyebrow his way.

"What? I made myself toast this morning. And I made a sandwich for lunch."

I gave him a playful punch in the arm. "Yeah, you're a regular Iron Chef."

He pulled me in for a warm kiss that melted away any worrying I might have had. When he finally pulled away, I was hotter than the microwaved chicken.

"I'm gonna grab a quick shower before dinner," he told me. Then as he walked away, he shot a wink over his shoulder. "Feel free to join me if you want."

I bit my lip, stared at the frozen food. Then made a beeline for the shower.

* * *

The next morning Ramirez woke up and was gone before dawn. The twins woke up colicky an hour later, and I woke up tired and still bathed in guilt over fleeing the murder scene and lying to my husband. I made a pot of coffee, fed both babies, and was just starting to feel human again when my cell buzzed to life on the counter. I grabbed it, checking the readout before I answered.

"Hey Dana," I grunted, my voice still gravelly with sleep. Or lack thereof.

"Seen the *Informer* this morning?" she asked, a hard edge in her voice usually used for yelling at her spin instructor.

Uh-oh.

"No..." I said, grabbing my laptop and tucking the phone under my chin as I pulled up the website.

There, splashed across the front page again, was Dana. This time Allie had somehow caught the two of us slurping down milkshakes at Foster's Freeze like they were going out of style. Above our images were the words "Dana Dashel Drowns in Dairy Delights."

I closed my eyes and thought a really dirty word. "Well, at least your hair looks great," I said.

"Did you read the headline!?"

I nodded. "She does have a thing for alliterations, doesn't she?"

"I'm going to kill her."

I didn't blame her. "I'll hold her down."

Dana sighed on the other end. "I can't live like this anymore. She's killing my career. Do you know what Lover Girl cosmetics did today?"

"What?" I asked, leaving the *Informer* and pulling up a Google screen.

"They asked if I was okay."

"And what did you tell them?"

"Well, that I was of course. But that's not the point. The point is they think I might *not* be okay."

"Well, you were photographed in Crocs."

"Oh, God, my career is over. Everyone in town thinks I've lost it. I'm going to be the laughing stock of Hollywood,"

"No you won't. No one will remember this in a day or two."

"Jennifer Aniston," she shot back. "No matter how happy she is now, she's always the girl Brad Pitt dumped. You know how many years ago that was?"

I shook my head at the phone. "Not really."

"Well, me neither. But it was at least five kids ago, if that gives you an idea of how long Hollywood's memory can be."

"I think you're overreacting just a little. I mean they just wanted to check on you," I told her as I scrolled through news stories, trying to see if there was any mention of our dead Russian.

"First the checking-on-you then the contract-dropping. I can't afford to lose Lover Girl, Maddie."

"Ah! Got it," I said, finding a story about the Bayshore Inn.

"Got what?" Dana asked.

"A story about our dead guy," I told her quickly scanning the article.

"What's it say?"

"That a body was found at the Bayshore. The guy's name was Vladimir Muskova. No mention of Irina or Katrina," I said, scanning the text. "The press must not have made the connection to the other murder yet."

"If there is one," Dana hedged.

"Oh, get this," I said, scrolling down the page. "He had a prior criminal record."

"For what?" Dana asked.

"I don't know. It doesn't say."

"I bet Ramirez could tell you."

I bit my lip. "I bet he could too. He'd also tell me to mind my own business and sleep on the couch tonight," I added.

"Right. Not the best option."

"Let me do a little more digging," I said, coming to the end of the article. "I'll call you back if I find anything."

Dana sighed, and I could hear her nodding on the other end. "Fine. I'll be here. With Allie stalking me, I'm not really in the mood to go out today anyway."

I made a few sympathetic sounds before hanging up. Max was fussing, so I dragged the laptop into the living room and set up camp on the floor between the babies' play mats. I typed with one hand while I dangled a stuffed elephant with sparkly ears just out of their reach.

Twenty minutes later, I was all googled out. I had completely exhausted any public internet records on one Vladimir Muskova.

My eyes strayed to an icon on my desktop. A police database Ramirez used when he did research from home. I did a quick angel-shoulder, devil-shoulder thing weighing the good of finding out the dead guy's connection to the dancing twins versus the bad of sneaking into my husband's files. Not surprisingly the dead Russian won out. I clicked the icon, doing a mental fist pump in the air when it turned out Ramirez's password was auto-saved, letting me right into the program.

I quickly typed my guy's name into the inquiry field, feeling like big red stop signs were going to flash on the screen at any minute, broadcasting proof of my intrusion to the entire L.A.P.D.

Luckily, the name spit out a record immediately. The database listed Vladimir Muskova, A.K.A. Vlad the Bad, as a smuggler. A smuggler of what, it didn't say, but he'd been arrested twice at the Canadian border, both times let go because of witnesses disappearing. I'd watched enough mob movies to know what that meant. I agreed with the nickname. Vlad was very bad.

I sat back, jiggling the elephant in Livvie's direction.

A smuggler visits Irina and fights with her. Then he visits Katrina. Then Katrina fights with her sister, and the sister ends up dead.

Then the smuggler ends up dead.

Were Katrina and Irina helping him smuggle something? Did something go wrong with the deal? If so, what? And who killed them? And how did buying votes on *Dancing with Celebrities* fit into all of this?

I didn't know. But I knew one thing. Of the three Russians, only one was still alive to answer my questions.

Katrina.

CHAPTER FIFTEEN

———

I called Mom, who was more than happy to take the twins again today. I dressed the gruesome twosome in matching outfits – Livvie in a pink, plaid ruffled dress with a ruffled diaper cover and Max in a blue plaid onesie with a pair of the most adorable teeny tiny denim jeans you ever saw – and loaded them into my minivan, dropping them, an enormous diaper bag, and enough milk to keep them fat and happy for the afternoon at Mom's house. Mom cooed and cuddled, and the twins giggled and gurgled back. I felt the slightest twinge that they all seemed perfectly happy to be spending the day without me. But I shoved it down, knowing that where I was going today was no place for kids.

My first stop was a two-story duplex off Wilshire, where I idled at the curb and texted number three on my speed dial. *out front. dbl parkd*

Five minutes later, Marco came flying out the front doors. "Dahling, I'm so glad you called me!" he sing-songed as he hopped into the car.

He wore a pair of jeans that looked painted onto his slim frame, rolled at the cuff to expose a pair of ankles that I'm pretty sure were smoother than mine. He had a sparkly red tank on top, a pair of woven sandals on his feet, and a bright fuchsia scarf tied around his neck. "Inconspicuous" was clearly not in Marco's vocabulary.

However, with Dana on the down-low today, I needed new backup. And sparkly was better than nothing.

An hour in traffic later we were in the Glitter Galaxy's parking lot, the nude woman on their sign flashing down at us.

Marco blinked, taking in his surroundings as I cut the engine. "Uh, Maddie. You said we were conducting interrogations today."

"I said *interviews*," I corrected him. "And we are."

"Then what are we doing here?"

"I need to talk to someone who works here."

Marco gulped, his Adam's apple bobbing up and down. "But, Maddie, it's a..." he leaned in, stage whispering. "...strip club."

"What tipped you off?" I asked, watching his face turn different shades of neon beneath the big, yellow nipple.

"There are naked people in there," Marco told me.

"I know."

"Naked *women*." He shuddered.

It took all I had not to laugh at him. Instead, I put a sympathetic hand on his arm. "Honey, it's going to be okay. Just stick close to me and avert your eyes from the stage."

Marco nodded. He got out of the minivan, glanced up at the yellow nipple, and visibly paled.

"You could wait in the car?" I suggested, taking pity on him.

He took a deep breath, squared his shoulders. "No. I can do this. You've seen one va-jay-jay, you've seen them all, right?" he said, doing a forced smile.

I paused. "*Have* you seen one va-jay-jay, Marco?"

He looked back up at the nude lady in neon. "Just hers," he squeaked out.

I patted him on the shoulder. "Be brave. They're not that bad."

He nodded, steeling himself for the worst as we entered the Glitter Galaxy.

The crowd was thicker than last time, though I noticed some of the same guys sitting in the same spots. I hoped they hadn't been here since yesterday.

Ling was on the stage, shaking her pint-sized derriere au natural in a pair of thigh-high white space boots and a pair of sparkly, glitter-covered alien antennae. And nothing else.

I thought I heard Marco gasp beside me.

"You okay?" I asked him.

He was staring wide-eyed at the woman on stage, the look on his face the same as if he'd been watching a tiger at the zoo devour a gazelle. "*This* is what you girls look like under your clothes?"

I glanced at Ling's tight abs and toned back-side, suddenly self-conscious about those few extra I-housed-two-people-for-nine-months inches of fat around my middle. "Well, we don't all look *exactly* like that."

"And men actually pay to see this?" he asked.

I nodded. "A surprising number," I mumbled.

He shuddered again. "I don't get it."

"Hey, you fellows aren't exactly adorable down there either," I pointed out.

He shot me an offended look. "At least I know my equipment. That looks like a mystery I'd never figure out."

I paused. "You know, there are a lot of straight guys that never do either."

I steered my shell-shocked friend toward a table in the back. Once I'd settled him in a seat with his back to the stage and a martini in his hand, he seemed to calm down some. Two songs later, Ling finished her set and exited the stage with several handfuls of bills in the top of her boots. I briefly contemplated a career change, noting that most of them were twenties.

"Be right back. I'm gonna go talk to Ling," I shouted to Marco as the strains of *Love in an Elevator* shot through the speakers, accompanying a blue, Na'vi painted girl who, as far as I could tell, was only wearing paint.

Marco took one look at the Avatar alien on stage and shook his head. "Nuh-uh, not without me, honey!" he called, grabbing his cocktail and following me.

I gave my name to a big, burly looking guy standing at the silver, beaded curtain beside the stage. He disappeared through it for just a minute, before returning with Ling.

"Hey, movie star friend, right?" she said, pointing at me.

I nodded. "Maddie."

"Sure, right. Hey, you find Kat yet?" she asked.

I shook my head in the negative. "No. But I'm still looking. I don't suppose you've seen her?"

"Sorry. She's still MIA." She paused, taking in my companion. "And this is...?"

"Marco," he said, giving her a limp handshake. "Party planner to the stars," he added.

"Oh, exciting. You do anyone I might know?"

"Well, I can't plan and tell," he hedged. "But let's just say that a certain host of a certain singing competition ending in the word 'Idol' has just had a birthday..."

Ling gasped. "You did his party?"

Marco nodded. "It was huge, honey."

"Oh." Ling nodded. "Very impressive. You know, I got a birthday coming up. Maybe I need a big party."

Marco clapped his hands in front of him. "Ooo, we could do a whole alien theme! I know this bakery that does the cutest little green cupcakes you ever saw. Cherry lime flavor. To die for!"

"Anyway," I jumped in, pulling us back on track. "Do you have any idea where Kat might have gone?" I asked Ling. "She ever talk about friends, family, anyone she might be staying with?"

Ling shook her head. "Not really. I mean, she was a hard girl to get to know. She really didn't have any close friends here. I mean, no one even really thought about it when she didn't show up for work. We all just kinda figured she got homesick and went back to Russia."

I nodded, though I was pretty sure that was not the case.

"But you know what I think now?" Ling said, narrowing her eyes.

"What?"

"I think maybe Kat was into something bad."

I bit my lip, not sure if I should tell her just how right I suspected she was. "Why do you say that?" I asked, instead.

"Well, you said her sister died. Then she disappears. Kinda funny, huh?"

"That's what we think, too!" Marco blurted out before I could stop him.

"So, you think Kat killed her sister then went on the lam?" she asked, pulling out another incongruent Americanism.

"I don't want to jump to conclusions," I hedged. "But I would like to speak to Kat. Do you know where she lives?" I asked.

Ling shrugged. "Sorry." She paused. "But I can look up her W9."

"Strippers pay taxes?" Marco asked.

"Sure. Government makes a pretty penny off of us, too. You know, I had to pay six figures in Schedule C taxes last year?"

I blinked. That's it, I was so in the wrong business. "You think her address might be on her employee records?" I asked.

Ling shrugged. "She had to put something down. I'll check it out if you wanna wait?"

"Please," I urged.

She nodded, then disappeared back into the silver, beaded curtain again. Ten minutes later Ling emerged, fully dressed. Or, at least dressed. She had on a micro-mini leather skirt, the same white go-go space boots, and a neon green tube top.

"I got her address," she said, waving a cocktail napkin above her head. "Let's go check on Kat."

"Let's?" I clarified.

"Hey, I wanna know what happened, too. This is the most exciting thing that's happened around here since that senator got caught wagging his Lyndon Johnson at Mindy in the back booth. Besides, my shift's over. Let's go. I'll buy lunch."

While I was pretty sure that adding a stripper to my entourage was not going to do much for my incognito factor, considering I'd emptied my purse at the Bayshore Inn yesterday, a free meal was a hard offer to pass up. Especially since I'd skipped breakfast.

"Okay. But I'm on a diet. We need diet food."

"Oh, I know just the place. It has a great salad bar," she said.

Fifteen minutes later we were at the Fresh Express soup, salad and pasta bar.

My growling stomach would have preferred a Double-Double with animal fries, but I was willing to settle for a salad smothered in bleu cheese dressing with a side of pasta and a baked potato. See how good I was being?

After we were fortified with carbs, fat, and, of course, some salad, we hopped back on the freeway and made our way to Burbank and the address on the cocktail napkin. Which turned out to be a rundown apartment building across the street from a Mailboxes N More shipping center and a liquor store. The studio neighborhood, this was not.

"I'm getting flashbacks," Ling said. "I used to live in a place like this when I first came to L.A. from Vietnam."

"Where do you live now?" I asked.

"Beverly Hills."

"Hey do you have to audition to be a stripper or do they let anyone do it?" I asked as we got out of the minivan.

Marco hit me in the arm.

"Ow. Just asking," I mumbled, rubbing the sore spot.

"Stripping is harder than it looks," Ling told me, popping a piece of gum into her mouth as she led the way up the walkway to the front of the building. "You have to have rhythm and timing and wax all over. It's a real pain in the butt."

"No pun intended," Marco snickered behind me.

The front door to the building was a simple glass thing, held together on the bottom by duct tape, which led to a small lobby done in vinyl wallpaper and red carpeting. Two doors were on the first floor, along with a stairway leading up. We took the stairs to the third floor where we found number 3E at the end of the hall.

I raised my hand and gingerly knocked. As I suspected, there was no response. I tried the handle. Locked.

"Now what?" Ling asked.

I glanced down the hall. Five other doors sat on this side and two more on the other. "Maybe her neighbors saw something? Maybe she told one of them where she was going?"

"Okay I'll take the doors on the left," Marco said, stepping up to 3D.

Ling took the ones on the right, and I opted to go talk to the downstairs neighbor. Having spent several years in a small apartment myself as a single lady, I knew that one man's ceiling was indeed another man's floor. Or, in our case, possible murderer's floor. Her downstairs neighbors may not have *seen* anything, but I'd bet money they'd heard Katrina on a regular basis.

I retraced my steps back into the stairwell, opening the metal fire door at the second floor and crossing the hallway to apartment 2E. I knocked. A beat later I heard footsteps shuffling to the door. After a short pause, a shadow crossed the peep-hole, then the door opened a crack.

A pair of dark eyes set in a mocha color face stared back at me. "What?"

I bit my lip. Not the most friendly greeting ever...

"Uh, hi. I'm a friend of Kat's," I said, stretching the truth farther than the elastic on Mrs. Rosenblatt's pants. "Your upstairs neighbor?"

The eyes just stared back.

"I haven't seen her in a few days and was wondering if maybe you knew where I could find her?"

"What am I, her babysitter?" The door opened further to reveal a middle-aged, African-American woman, her hair in curlers, a housecoat that looked like it belonged in a fifties sitcom around her, and a pair of slippers on her feet that appeared to be shedding pink yarn.

"No. Clearly not," I backtracked. "I just wondered if maybe you'd heard anything lately. Like Kat's footsteps. Has she been home?"

The woman shook her head. "Thank God. That thing sounded like she was tap dancin' on my ceiling every night. I told her to keep it down one day, and you know what she said to me?"

I shook my head.

"Told me to 'mind your business fatso'", the woman said, doing air quotes. "You believe that bitch? Bringing my glandular condition into it."

"She sounds like a real peach," I said, sympathetically. "But you said it's been silent lately?"

She nodded. "That's right."

"When was the last time you heard her?"

She shook her head. "Sorry. I didn't notice. I figured maybe she's been stayin' with her boyfriend."

"Kat had a boyfriend?" I said, jumping on the info.

"That's what I assumed. I mean, from the way they was arguing, they had to be dating."

"You heard arguing? With a man?"

She nodded again. "Yep. Lots. Just before the tap dancing stopped actually."

"What did they say?"

"No idea," she said, shaking her head. "Alls I heard was loud yellin' in some foreign language."

"You didn't happen to see the boyfriend, did you?" I asked.

She shook her head. "Sorry. I don't pry," she said, giving me a look like she thought I shouldn't either.

I took that as my cue to leave and thanked her.

I bit my lip as I digested this new info. So Vlad had caught up to Katrina both at the club *and* here at home. Then Irina shows up dead and so does he. Did Katrina kill them both? And, if so, where was she now?

I was still letting my sleep-deprived brain mull those questions over as I stepped into the stairwell again. The fire door closed behind me with a bang as I trudged up the flight of stairs back to the third floor.

I got halfway up when I heard a sound behind me. Metal on the metal stairs, echoing off the walls.

I froze, my heart racing.

"Hello?" I called out.

But I got nothing in response except my own breath coming fast.

I was being paranoid. It was a big building. Busy. Any number of people could be in the stairwell at any time.

Ignoring how dark and isolated the stairwell suddenly felt, I quickly ran up the remaining steps. My hand was just on the doorknob to the third floor exit when I heard the sound behind me again.

This time much closer.

I spun around to see what it was.

But I was too late.

Before I could register any visual, pain exploded behind my left ear, my vision went blurry, and I watched the stairs at my feet rush up to meet me.

Then everything went black.

CHAPTER NINETEEN

———

I was lying in the softest bed imaginable. Feather pillows on top of feather pillows, surrounded by big, downy comforters and fluffy blankets. I was warm, cozy, and even snoring just a little. I was wearing the same pink flannel pajamas with white bunnies on them that I'd had in second grade. They smelled like fabric softener and milk chocolate. I burrowed deeper into my fluffy, warm nest feeling completely rested.

Which should have been my first clue I was dreaming. It had been exactly one-hundred and two days since I'd had enough sleep to feel anything even close to rested. (But who was counting?)

"Maddie!" I heard someone call my name. Faintly at first, just the mildest irritation to my peaceful slumber world, like a buzzing gnat in my peripheral. "Maddie! Speak to me, Maddie!" Then it became louder, more insistent, accompanied by a jarring motion that shook my brain against my skull in pounding waves.

"Uhn," I responded, grunting at my interruption.

"She's alive!" I heard someone else yell.

I slowly blinked one eye open, grunting again as the sudden onslaught of glaring light slammed against my brain.

Marco's face hovered over mine, his drawn-in eyebrows curved in a V of concern.

"Ohmigod, Maddie, speak to me, honey. Don't go toward the light!"

If it didn't hurt so much, I would have rolled my eyes. "I'm not going toward anything."

"She's fine," I heard Ling's accented voice in the background. "Just a little bump. I've gotten worse falling off the pole."

My hand went to the back of my head, feeling a large lump forming there. "What happened?" I asked, still blinking. My head hammered like I'd been indulging in margaritas but without the fun buzz first.

"We heard a sound in the stairwell. Then when we got here, we found you on the floor. Unconscious!" Marco yelled, grabbing me up in a hug. "I thought I'd lost you, dahling."

While the over-drama was crushing the air out of me, the sentiment was touching.

"I'm fine," I said, disentangling myself from his clutches. Which was close to the truth, I realized as I wiggled my limbs, one at a time. My knee was growing a bruise, and my nose was scraped raw from meeting the sharp steps. And my head hurt. But nothing felt broken or beyond repair.

"Someone hit me," I told them.

Ling gasped. "You were attacked? I knew this neighborhood was no good."

I agreed. But I didn't think there was anything random about this particular attack.

"Did you see the guy?" Marco asked.

I shook my head. "I heard someone. But he hit me before I could see his face." I paused. "Or hers." While someone had packed quiet a punch, it could easily have been male or female. I closed my eyes again, rubbing my temples, trying to remember anything I could from right before the attack. I'd heard footsteps, sensed a presence. But that was about it. No tell-tale perfume smells or limping gait like in the movies. In real life, being hit on the head was far less glamorous or helpful.

"Come on, let's get out of here," Marco said, helping me to my feet. I didn't protest, leaning on him as I gingerly put weight on my bruised knee. It felt like someone had kicked me hard, but it held. I hobbled down the two flights of stairs to the first floor, leaning on Marco's shoulders as Ling held the doors. Then we all hightailed it back to my minivan where Marco hopped behind the wheel. After dropping Ling back at Glitter

Galaxy, he drove me home, where he insisted on carrying me into the house.

"I can walk," I protested as he groaned under my weight.

"No. (pant) It's okay. (pant) I can do it. (pant, pant) You're light as a (pant) feather."

"Are you being sarcastic?" I asked him.

"Who me? Never."

I wasn't sure I believed him, but seeing as he was playing nursemaid, I let it go.

He set me down with a jostling thud on the sofa, then made up a hot pack for my neck, a cold pack for my knee, and a compress for my head. He made tea, got aspirin, and elevated my leg on a pillow. I had to admit, it was kind of nice being the one babied for a change. Even though the aspirin and cold pack were making my head feel better at a rapid rate, I let him continue his dramatic ministrations for another half hour until I finally felt ready to take on the twins and texted Mom to bring them home.

I did my best to hide my injuries from her as she and Mrs. R dropped two miraculously sleeping babies in their cribs. Amazingly, she ignored my hobble, quickly rushing back out the door, saying she was five minutes away from winning a hot eBay bidding war on a discount designer purse.

I was just ushering Marco out the door, assuring him for the umpteenth time that I was not hovering near death, when Ramirez's SUV pulled up in the driveway.

I took a deep breath, shoved the cold packs back in the fridge, and ran for the bathroom where I applied an extra layer of make-up to the scrape on my nose.

"Hey, babe, you home?" I heard my husband yell from the front door.

"Yeah. In here," I called back, giving myself a once over. The scrape was better, but still visible. I added some powder on top.

"Hey," Ramirez said, peeking his head around the doorframe. "Babies sleeping?"

I nodded, ducking my head down. "Amazing, right?"

"You have the magic touch."

I cringed. Actually, my Mom had the magic touch. My touch seemed to inspire howls lately. But I glossed over the details. "How was your day?" I asked.

"Good. Long," he answered, turning back toward the living room.

I followed behind him, only slightly limping, hoping he didn't turn around.

"Make any progress on Ricky's case?" I asked as he flopped onto the sofa. I sat down next to him, snuggling into the crook of his arm. Both because it was a pretty sweet place to snuggle and because he couldn't very well see my nose from that angle.

Ramirez shrugged in answer to my question. "I guess."

"Oh? New developments?"

Ramirez shot me a look. "No. Contrary to what you see on TV," he said, gesturing toward the offending object, "real police work is about following up on evidence. A new breaking twist doesn't happen at every commercial break."

"Geeze, lay off the TV, huh? What did TV ever do to you?"

He grinned. "Sorry. Like I said, long day."

"I feel you." Boy, did I feel for him on that score.

"I don't suppose you have dinner plans?" Ramirez asked.

I bit my lip. "Weight Watchers low cal chicken teriyaki?"

He groaned. "If I tell you that you look hot and skinny, can we have lasagna?"

I swatted his arm. "*You* can have whatever you like."

Ramirez raised a hopeful eyebrow my way. "Really?"

"Uh-huh. As long as you cook it."

"I knew there was a catch." He sighed. "All right. I guess I'm having sandwiches again." He slapped my knee as he got up.

I bit my lip to stifle a wince at the pain.

"You sure you don't want lasagna?" he asked again, disappearing into the kitchen.

"I'm sure!" I called out, breathing through my mouth as the pain in my bruised knee subsided.

I leaned my head back on the sofa. This lying thing was so not my style.

* * *

If ever there was a day I would have loved to sleep in, the next one was it. Unfortunately, sleeping-in was a foreign concept to the twins, who started their dueling wails before dawn. I dragged myself out of bed, noticing that the other side was already empty, and shuffled into the nursery, systematically changing one baby, then the other. (Then the first one again, as he spit up on his blue, teddy-bear clad suit.) I settled them both into their swings, warming up two bottles and simultaneously feeding them. Then I made a really big pot of coffee and took two more aspirins.

As I shuffled into the bathroom and looked at myself in the mirror I realized what a fortunate thing it was that my husband had taken off early again. The scraped nose had taken on a purple hue and was swollen like Marsha Brady. I slapped more foundation on it, a layer of powder, then some bronzer to even it all out. I contemplated a shower but considering the fussy state of the twosome this morning, I opted for a double layer of deodorant, mascara, and hair spray instead. I climbed into a white, denim skirt and a baby-doll T, and by the time Dana showed up at my front door, I was looking mostly presentable.

Mostly.

"Ohmigod, your nose!" Dana cried.

My hand flew immediately to my face. "Is it that bad? I tried to cover it up."

"It looks like you went ten rounds with Mike Tyson."

"No, just one round with a flight of stairs," I told her, running back to the bathroom for more cover-up. As I dabbed it on, I told her about the trip to Katrina's apartment and the attack on the stairwell."

"You think it was the same person who killed Irina and Vlad?" she asked when I'd finished.

I shrugged. "If I had to guess? Yes." I paused, checking my reflection. "How's this look?"

Dana squinted at my nose. "It looks like you need more cover-up."

"It's already caked on as thick as I can get it."

"I've got some stuff at home," Dana said. "I'll go grab it. It's a new Lover Girl product. The stuff is like silly putty; it covers anything."

"You're a lifesaver."

"So you didn't get a look at him? The guy that did this?" Dana asked.

I shook my head. "Or girl," I amended.

"You think it was Katrina?"

"Who else would be hanging around her apartment building?"

"Good point," Dana agreed. "I don't suppose any of the neighbors knew where Katrina went?"

I shook my head, relaying what Marco and Ling had told me on the ride home. "No. The woman next door said she heard arguing, just like the downstairs neighbor. But no one knows where Katrina went afterwards. She wasn't particularly close with anyone. They all said she had a temper and kept to herself."

"Just like Irina," Dana mused. "You know, I wonder... they both seemed to want to keep their private lives very private."

I nodded. "True."

"I mean, Irina didn't even want people to know she had a sister."

"Right..." I said, my tired brain trying to play catch-up to wherever Dana was going with this.

"So, why would she risk bringing Vlad on the set? I mean, it's clear to just about everyone on the show that there's a press leak. So, she must have had a really good reason. I mean, she could have easily arranged buying votes over the phone. Why have Vlad there in person?"

I bit my lip. "Great question."

One I was still pondering when my cell buzzed to life in my pocket. I pulled it out to find a text from Mom.

u up? big ebay find

Oy. I was going to have to stage a fashion intervention for her at some point.

I'm up I texted back.

As soon as I hit "send" my cell rang, Mom's number flashing. I stabbed the on button.

"Hey, Mom."

"Maddie, you'll never guess what I found on eBay this morning."

"Half price tie to go with the Armani?"

I could hear her shaking her head. "No! Dancing shoes!"

Mental forehead smack. "Mom, please tell me you're not taking up tap dancing."

"Not tap, Maddie. They are ballroom dancing shoes. Gorgeous shoes, too. Purple, suede, little kitten heels."

I raised an eyebrow. I was impressed. Usually my Mom wore only flats and mules. The fact she knew a kitten from a wedge was a sign there was hope for her after all.

"Anyway, the reason I'm calling is it may relate to your investigation," she continued. "The listing says that they're shoes worn by Irina on *Dancing with Celebrities*."

I perked up, suddenly giving Mom my full attention. "Wait, are these the shoes she did the tango in?" I clarified. "With little blue rhinestones down the sides?"

"Yes! It says they're authentic, but I'm not sure how that could be. I mean, don't they usually keep the wardrobe on the set?"

Usually they did. But, as I well knew, these particular shoes had been the first item to go missing from the DWC set.

And now I knew just where they were.

"I'll be right over," I told her. "Don't let anyone outbid you!"

CHAPTER SEVENTEEN

———

Half an hour later Dana had run home for the latest and greatest Lover Girl had to offer, I had assured my mom that even though I looked like a prize fighter (and a losing one, at that) her "baby" was okay, and the twins had shouted in gleeful unison at the sight of their favorite babysitter. I tried to tune out the guilty feeling that brought on, instead directing my attention to my mom's computer screen. There, in front of me, were the purple, suede, strappy ballroom shoes with rhinestones down the side that Irina had worn two weeks ago. So far, the bidding was up to $346 dollars, with the auction set to end in just seventy-two minutes. There was no doubt about it. We'd found Lana's missing wardrobe piece.

And after checking the name of the eBay seller - DWCKat12 - I had a pretty good idea who had taken them.

"So it was Irina's sister that was stealing from the set all along," Mrs. R said. "No wonder she argued with her sister."

She was a possible murderer, she'd hit me over the head, and she was a thief. I was beginning to like Katrina less and less.

"How do we find out where she is?" I asked Mom, scanning the page for info. The item location was listed as Los Angeles, California, but that didn't narrow things down a whole lot.

"You could try clicking on her name," Mom instructed me.

I did, a page about DWCKat12 coming up. Unfortunately it had scant info. She had been a seller for only three months, had a 4 star approval rating, with two reviews stating that they had experienced "fast shipping." I narrowed my eyes at the previous reviews. What did you want to bet they were for purchases of a sequined waltz headpiece and a sparkly gown in a men's fifty-six long.

"Is there any way to contact the seller?" I asked, scanning the page.

I felt Mom nod behind me. "Sure. You can send an email." She pointed to a contact link.

I pursed my lips. "I'm not sure that will help." What were the chances that Katrina would confess all in an email via eBay's messaging system? "What about a phone number or address?"

Mom shook her head this time. "No. eBay won't give out personal information. Trust me, I've tried. I had this guy sell me a 'designer' scarf," she said, doing air quotes around the word with her index fingers. "Turns out it was a knock-off from China. I contacted eBay every which way to get my money back, but all they could do was flag his account. I never saw a dime."

Mrs. Rosenblatt nodded. "Sometimes a deal is just too good to be true."

I clicked back to the eBay listing page, watching the counter for the auction to wind down to sixty-eight minutes now.

I sat back in my chair chewing my lower lip. "Okay, let's say that Irina lets her twin onto the set of DWC. Katrina is jealous that Irina is a star while she's dancing the pole at the Glitter Galaxy. So Kat sees an opportunity to make a little money. She starts stealing items from the set and sells them on eBay. Irina finds out, she kills Irina."

"But where does the smuggler come in?" Mom asked.

I narrowed my eyes at the screen. "Good question." And one I intended to ask Katrina as soon as I got my hands on her.

"What happens if we bid?" I asked Mom.

She shot me a look. "Seriously, Maddie, you've never used eBay?" She tsked at my lack of internet skills, shaking her head back and forth.

"I prefer to shop in person. It's a whole sensory experience, the smells of the new clothes, the feel of the fabric, the sound of the register dinging back at me as my credit card is accepted."

Mom smiled at me. "You're so cute."

"Okay, so enlighten me. What happens if I put a bid in for the shoes?"

"Well, its pretty simple. If you're the high bidder at the end, you get them."

"Perfect." I leaned forward, typing in an amount in the little "bid now" box.

"Wait!" Mom shouted, her hand shooting out and grabbing the mouse from me. "You can't bid *now*!" she told me.

I gave her a blank look.

"If you bid now, the other bidders will just bid again, too," she explained. "You're only driving the price up."

I looked down at the listing. The screen showed that eight other bids have been placed already. The current high bidder was bunhead89.

"So, how do I win?"

"You wait until the last second," Mrs. Rosenblatt jumped in. "When the clock starts counting down, you swoop in with a bid that's so high the others won't have time to outbid you before the clock runs out."

I had the distinct impression I was in the presence of eBay shopping masters, so I took their advice. Instead of bidding, I made a fresh pot of coffee, changed the babies' diapers, and did some very productive pacing as I watched the auction timer tick down the minutes.

At thirty-seven minutes Dana showed up at the front door. I opened it to find her dressed in a head to toe silver sheath with Swarovski crystals along one side and a pair of Louboutins in hot pink on her feet.

I blinked. "Please tell me you have a red carpet event to go to this afternoon?"

Dana breezed past me. "No. Why?"

"'Why?' Have you looked in the mirror?"

"Oh, this old thing," she said, waving me off.

"You're in a thousand dollar dress."

Dana pursed her lips. "Okay, look: I figure if we're hot on Katrina's trail, so is Allie Quick. If she's going to photo-stalk me, I want to look fabulous, okay? No more pics of me stuffing my face or wearing shlumpy sweats."

She had a point. "Got the cover-up?" I asked.

She handed me a beige tube. "It's the thickest stuff money can buy."

I hoped so as I took the tube into the bathroom and squeezed out a generous helping. Almost immediately it started to dry into a thick paste. I rubbed it along my nose. The consistency reminded me of bubble gum, but as I sculpted it onto my swollen features, I had to admit, it did the trick. I looked almost normal. Slightly larger than usual, but the purple was covered.

"So what's happening on eBay?" Dana asked.

I quickly filled her in about the auction. Then we all hovered around the computer again, watching the countdown.

At fifteen minutes, my palms started to sweat. Max had a poopy diaper, and I changed it faster than I have ever changed before, coming back to the screen just as it flipped over to five minutes.

"Should we bid now?" I asked. "It's getting close."

"No!" Mom yelled. "You have to be strong. Wait until the last minute."

"The *very* last minute," Mrs. R said, nodding sagely beside her.

I bit my lip. I felt sweat break out along my spine as I watched the numbers count down. I bobbed my knee up and down with nervous energy. This was our only connection to Katrina and the last chance to find out what really happened to Irina. If I didn't win this bid, we were sunk. "How about now?" I asked at a minute-thirty.

"Wait," Mom instructed me.

I did, my fingers hovering over the keyboard. Anxiety was jumping in my belly like a five-year-old in a bounce house.

"And… now!" Mom yelled.

"Go, go, go," Mrs. R shouted in my ear.

I did, fingers fumbling as I typed in $379.

"No! Maddie, you can't bid that!" Mom screamed.

Forty-five seconds to go.

"Why? What did I do wrong?"

"Quickly! Change it! Higher!"

Thirty-six seconds.

I did, striking the "delete" key with such force, I was afraid it might pop off. I put in $400.

"No round numbers!" Mom shrieked.

Delete, delete, delete.

Twenty-two seconds.

"Hurry!" Dana cried at me.

"Move over, let me do it," Mom instructed.

I did, sliding out of the chair, and bouncing up and down on my tip-toes as I watched her fingers fly across the keyboard. She typed in the amount of her bid. $1769.

I almost swallowed my tongue.

"I can't pay that!?"

"You won't have to. Trust me," Mom said, hitting "commit to buy."

I closed my eyes doing a silent prayer to the Paypal gods that she was right.

Eight seconds.

We all leaned forward, breath held, eyes bulging, the tension in the air so thick you could cut it with a stiletto heel.

A bar appeared next to the price, stating that I was the high bidder.

I sucked in a breath, crossed my fingers, toes, and legs.

Then with five seconds left, the price changed.

"What's going on?" I asked, panic in my voice.

"Bun Head is trying to outbid us," Mom told me.

"Will she?"

She shook her head. "Not likely. Not with my number."

I watched the price climb as she tried to outbid me. $467. $492. $512.

Three seconds, two seconds, one… the screen flashed, and the auction ended.

I held my breath as the screen changed.

Then a notice appeared telling me that I was the high bidder and had agreed to purchase the shoes for $539.

I let out an audible sigh of relief. Dana whooped so loudly the twins started crying again. Mrs. R did a war cry. And Mom just smiled. "See, I told you I knew what I was doing."

I wrapped my arms around her neck in a hug. "You rock."

She beamed even bigger. "Thanks." She clicked on the "pay now" button. "Now, how do you want to pay?"

I only cringed slightly at paying $539 for the stolen shoes, clicking on the "overnight shipping" option at checkout.

"What are you going to do with them?" Dana asked.

"It's not what I'm doing with them," I said, following the procedure on the screen to check out. "It's what I'm going to do with the person who now has to ship these shoes to me."

* * *

An hour later Dana, Mom, Mrs. Rosenblatt, and the twins, in their matching car seats, were all strapped into my seven passenger minivan, staked out across the street from the Mailboxes N More shop facing Katrina's apartment building.

"Are you sure she'll show up?" Dana asked, crossing her legs awkwardly in the minimal room in my backseat to keep her gown from wrinkling.

I shook my head. "Honestly? No. But it's my best guess."

She nodded. "What do we do when she does?"

That was the part of the plan I hadn't gotten to yet.

The twins started to cry in the back. Two rounds of "Where is Thumbkin", two bottles, two battles with Mom over just how many blankets babies needed in eighty-degree L.A. heat, and one stinky diaper change done in my trunk later, a beat-up Chevy Malibu pulled up to the mailboxes store, and a woman got out. She was tall and slim, with dark hair and exotic eyes. The spitting image of Irina.

I heard Dana suck in a breath behind me. "It's her!"

I agreed. The similarity was too much not to be her. It was almost eerie, like seeing Irina's ghost. She was dressed in a skin-tight, spandex skirt, platform heels, and a tank top - all done in various colors of cheetah print.

I watched as she pulled a shoebox-sized package from her backseat and walked into the mailboxes store. Five minutes later, she walked out again, minus the shoebox, and got back into the Malibu.

"Follow her!" Mom yelled.

I did, putting the minivan into gear and pulling out onto the street behind her. I followed her parallel to the 134, then watched her turn right onto a side street. I did the same, catching up to her as she pulled into traffic on Verdugo. I lost her at a red light a block later, my knee jiggling up and down as I waited for it to turn. When it did, I jumped forward, scanning the cars ahead for any sign of her.

"There, there!" Dana shouted pointing to our left. The Malibu turned down another side street. I cursed, pulling around the block as quickly as the traffic would allow and cutting across at the next intersection.

At first I thought we'd lost her again. But then I heard Mrs. R yell from the backseat, "There, on the left!"

Sure enough, three cars ahead on the left was the Malibu. I surged forward in traffic, and a second later I was smack dab behind the it.

It wasn't the most stealthy move, but with L.A. traffic the chances of her spotting us were still slim. Besides, I wasn't real keen on the idea of a high speed chase with my twins strapped in the back of the car.

I held onto her bumper for a full five more miles down Burbank, heading east toward the Inland Empire before she pulled into a parking lot and cut the engine. It was a mini mall with an outdoor array of shops, dress barns, and discount shoe stores.

I followed Kat's lead, parking three spots down, watching as she got out of the car and headed toward one of the shops.

"Now what?" Dana asked.

"Let's go after her!" Mrs. R shouted.

I swiveled in my seat, looking at my motley crew. I had a movie starlet dressed for the red carpet, a three-hundred pound woman in a neon green muumuu, a pair of fussy three month old twins, and my mom, who was wearing faded jeans pulled almost up to her armpits and a sweater with a Scotty dog printed on the front. Incognito, we were not.

"Let's wait," I suggested. "She's got to come out sometime."

I could tell Mrs. R was itching to do some cloak and dagger moves, but when I offered to hit the drive-thru McDonald's on the corner, I got agreement from everyone. Well, almost everyone. Livvie started to cry, but Dana popped a binky into her mouth and all was well.

Three frosty milkshakes and one no-sugar iced tea later (Guess who the iced tea was for. God, I hated dieting!), we were all making slurping sounds with our straws in the parking lot, once again parked three slots down from the Malibu when Katrina made her return.

I shot bolt upright, almost spilling my iced tea.

"There she is," Mom said. "Follow her!"

Again, I did, turning over the engine as she pulled out of her space and back onto the road. I waited a beat, trying to stay back a car length while still keeping her in sight this time. Which wasn't easy as the noontime drivers had cleared considerably, and we were now in much sparser traffic. I hung back, following her north this time, along North Hollywood Way, then watched as she turned onto a side street that ran between two large apartment buildings. I made a sharp right behind her, following her at as safe a distance as I could while still keeping her in sight.

"Hurry, she's getting away!" Dana urged.

"Can't. Speed limit is 35 here," I told her.

She leaned forward in her seat and shot me a look like I'd grown two heads. "You're kidding, right?"

"I have to be careful. I have babies on board!" I said, gesturing to the diamond shaped sign suctioned to my back window as proof.

Dana rolled her eyes at me.

Another left, then a right, and I pulled onto Victory just in time to see the Malibu's taillights sail through a yellow light.

"Sonofa-," I stopped myself just in time as I hit the brakes on the red. I watched the Malibu go a block down, then make another right. I tapped my fingers in anticipation on the steering wheel. "Come on, come on, come on," I encouraged the light. Finally it changed to green, and I hit the gas with such force, Mrs. R surged backward in her seat, almost toppling over.

"Sorry," I called to my passengers, chasing after the Malibu and making the sharp right like I'd seen her do.

Only I realized two things as I turned the corner and the next street came into view. One: that as we had engaged in our very safe, low speed chase along surface streets, we'd wound our way north, almost to the 5. And two: losing Katrina along a back road was the least of our problems. Because I knew exactly where she was going.

"Oh no," I said out loud, as I watched Katrina's taillights pull to the right, past the Bob Hope Metrolink Station.

Leading right into the Burbank airport.

CHAPTER EIGHTEEN

――――――

"Ohmigod, she's making a run for it," Dana said, realization hitting her too as the big, bold "Welcome to the Burbank Airport" sign came into view.

While "run" might not be the accurate word for the speed her car was going through the terminal, the sentiment fit. Clearly Kat was taking the money and leaving town. My money, to be exact.

We watched her pull into long term parking, though I had a sneaking suspicion that she had no plans to pick up her junker car again later. I followed her, pulling into a slot two rows over as I watched her get out of the car, pop her trunk, and pull out a suitcase big enough to fit my entire shoe collection in.

"She doesn't look like she's going on an overnighter," Mrs. R remarked.

I nodded. "No kidding."

"So, what are we waiting for? Let's go after her," Mom said, hand on the door handle.

I paused. While I didn't want to let our one and only suspect get away, the last thing I wanted to do was expose my babies to a woman who was at best a thief and at worst a cold blooded killer who'd murdered her own twin. Plus, the babies were asleep. Everyone knows you *never* wake a sleeping baby.

"You guys stay here. I'll go stop her," I told Mom and Mrs. R.

Mom's eyes cut to the babies. She nodded, as if understanding my motivation.

"I'm going with you," Dana said, hopping out of the van in her couture gown before I could stop her. "You might need backup."

There was no "might" about it. I totally needed backup. While it was reasonably safe to assume that Katrina wasn't carrying a weapon with her into a high security airport, as I knew from my past experience with her, it didn't take a gun to put someone down.

I left the keys with Mom, and Dana and I quickly made up time, following in Katrina's footsteps from the long term parking lot to the short line of terminals. While Burbank was a busy airport, it was nowhere near the size of LAX. Burbank was the locals' choice for easy commuter flights, servicing mostly flights going to west coast hubs. It was a domestic airport, meaning Kat wasn't making her international run from Burbank. But with the amount of international hubs that Burbank connected to, it was also an easy way out of town. I knew for a fact from my days at the Art Institute, that several flights a day went between Burbank and San Francisco, which was an easy connection to anywhere overseas.

Dana and I hung back as Katrina got in line behind a group of girls in volleyball uniforms at the Delta counter. And we might have done a bang-up job of blending in with the other travelers, too, had Dana not looked fresh from the red carpet.

"Ohmigod, ohmigod," a chubby, short teen guy in a *Moonlight* T-Shirt yelled. "I know you! You're Dana Dashel!"

"Uh… no?" Dana said. "I'm not?"

"Ohmigod, I totally loved you in that HBO series, *Lady Justice*! You are, like, the hottest lawyer I've ever seen."

"Um, thanks," Dana said, keeping her voice low. "But I'm not really a lawyer-"

But Super Fan didn't take the hint. "I am so sorry about Ricky!" he went on. "I totally know he's, like, innocent. I mean, hello? He's a movie star."

The fanboy moment was attracting a crowd. A couple at the next ticket counter turned and stared, and a family of four was pointing and whispering. In the waiting lounge, heads were turning, and I saw three tween girls pop up from their chairs and get a running start toward us.

I whipped my head around to the Delta counter.

Katrina was staring straight at us.

I swallowed hard, watching her take in the scene, then quickly turn on her heels and head toward the departure gates.

If she made it past security, there was no way we'd catch her.

I thought of alerting one of the many security personnel milling in the area, but so far all we had her on was selling stolen goods on eBay. And I didn't even have proof of that; she'd just mailed it to me. I wasn't sure that my say-so was the level orange kind of risk these guys would care about.

"Can you sign my chest?" Super Fan asked, shoving a sharpie at Dana and pulling up his shirt to expose a pair of pimply man boobs.

Dana's eyes shot from the chest to me to Katrina's departing back. She mouthed the words, "Go. I'll catch up."

I did, quickly following Katrina.

Katrina turned, saw me approaching, and took off at a run. She knocked into a couple with carry-ons, narrowly avoided a magazine rack, then ducked into the women's restroom. I chased after her, hitting the door just as a large Asian family emerged. I navigated around them and was confronted with dozens of shiny, metal stalls.

I paused. Katrina could be in any one of them. A woman in a heavy scarf stood at the mirror, applying lipstick. An executive type in a blazer and A-line skirt was adding tap water to a bottle full of powered drink mix. And a teenager with spiked hair was washing her hands.

Behind them, flushing, paper being rolled.

I ducked down, checking out the shoes in the first stall. Loafers. Not our girl.

I duck-walked down the line, peeking under the doors of each closed stall. Sandals. Uggs. Flip flops. Pumps.

Then I hit pay dirt.

Hot pink cheetah printed platforms.

I stood and put my ear to the door (incurring a funny look from the executive type at the sink in the process). Silence.

"Katrina?" I asked.

Nothing.

"I know you're in there."

Again, silence.

"You can't hide forever."

Still no response.

"I know you stole the shoes-" I started, but before I could finish, the metal door slammed open, hitting me squarely in the nose.

"Uhn." I staggered backward, pain exploding behind my eyes as the full force of Katrina's dancer body slammed into me while she bolted past.

I recovered just in time to grab a handful of her tank-top, yanking her backward.

She yelled, a short yip, stumbling on her platforms and twisting to the right. She pushed me backward, into the bathroom stall. I tripped, falling butt first into the toilet.

"Ew!" I cried, feeling the back side of my skirt get soaked. I jumped up, regaining my footing, just as she made a break for the door.

I scrambled after her, and flew out of the restroom just in time to see her pull open a service door next to a taco restaurant, disappearing behind it. I chased after her, my wet skirt slapping against my thighs. I slipped through the service door to find myself in a long, slim corridor, with several doorways leading off in both directions.

I paused, listening to my own breath echo off the concrete walls. No footsteps. No sign of Katrina.

"Katrina?" I yelled, the silence deafening. I took a tentative step forward. Then another.

I was halfway down, when a blur of cheetah flew at me from a doorway.

"Uhn." I heard myself grunt as the weight of her body took me down to the floor. But this time I held onto her, arms wrapping around her middle as she tried to wiggle free.

"Let go," she screamed at me.

"No way. You have my five-hundred and thirty-nine dollars."

She paused, her eyes narrowing. "What are you talking about?"

"I'm talking about the money you sold the stolen DWC shoes for on eBay!"

Katrina sucked in a breath. "You're bargainbaby49?"

"I am, and you're busted."

"Hey, I was conducting a legitimate sale," she protested, wriggling in my grasp. "If you have an issue with it, contact eBay."

"A sale of items you stole," I pressed, holding tight. "Irina got you onto the *Dancing with Celebrities*, then you stole wardrobe items to sell on eBay."

"I don't know what you're talking about," she protested.

"I think you do. I also think your sister found out about it, and you killed her."

"No!" Katrina shouted, breaking from my grasp and struggling to her knees.

"Yes!" I yelled, pulling at a handful of her hair.

She grunted. "You have it all wrong, you stupid beetch," she said. "I didn't steal the items. Irina did."

I'll admit, that tidbit threw me. So much that I involuntarily loosened my grip, allowing Katrina to struggle away and gain the upper hand. She lunged at me again, straddling me on the ground. One cheetah platform sailed toward my jugular. I reacted without thinking, shoving my purse between her heel and my throat just in time.

"Why would Irina steal from her own show?" I choked out.

"She needed the money."

"What they were paying on DWC wasn't enough?" I asked, turning to the side, and slipping out from under her foot. I scrambled to my hands and knees.

"No!" Kat shouted, her hand shooting out to get a grip on my ankle. "Irina didn't see any big money unless she won."

"Which is why she was trying to rig the votes," I added, puzzle pieces falling into place.

"It was a stupeed idea," Katrina said, using her favorite word again. "Too risky. The producers were bound to find out. And Vladimir agreed with me."

"Vladimir Muskavo," I said, kicking at her hand with my other heel. "So you were working together?"

Her face scrunched up. "Working together? No!" She spit on the ground and cursed in Russian. "He was a snake, a fiend, the worst kind of man."

I kicked free, getting as far as my knees before Katrina pounced again, growling under her breath as she grabbed me from behind.

"I don't get it then," I said, straining away from her. "If you weren't working with him, what was your connection to Vlad?"

"Irina and I had to get out of our hometown. You have no idea what it's like there. Where we come from, women are dogs. They can marry American or be prostitute. That's all."

While it sounded horrible, I had a hard time conjuring up sympathy for her while she had her arms wrapped around my throat. "But you did get out. Two years ago," I said, quoting Irina's official bio.

I felt Katrina nod behind me. "We did. We paid big money to a man to smuggle us out of the country."

Puzzle piece! "Vladimir." He wasn't smuggling stolen goods *out* of the country, he was smuggling people *in*.

Katrina nodded again. "We paid him a large sum of money to get us into the country through Canada. He provided us with new names, passport, everything we needed to make it look like we belonged here."

"But that was two years ago," I pointed out, twisting to my right, breaking her grip to face her. "Why was he here now?"

Katrina pulled away, panting. "Because of my stupeed sister," she said. Then she spit on the ground again. "She has some big idea to be a famous dancer. She goes on TV. Lets the whole world see her!"

"Including Vladimir," I said, starting to get the big picture.

"Yes. He said that if we didn't pay him more money, he would turn her in to immigration, and they would send us both back to Russia."

"So that's when Irina came up with the idea of fixing the votes to win the money."

Karina shook her head. "Yes, but Vlad wanted money now."

"So when trying to fix the votes didn't pay off soon enough, Irina started stealing items from the set to sell," I said.

Katrina nodded. "This was my plan," she said, beaming with pride. "People will pay big money for TV memorabilia."

"So what went wrong?"

Her eyes flashed. "Vlad was greedy. We sold one item and gave him the money, but he wanted more. He said we had to bring him to set to steal things. He said he could make big bucks smuggling all kinds of equipment off the set and selling to Canadian production companies."

"But Irina was against it, and they argued," I concluded.

"She knew the producers would figure it out. That's why he must have killed her." Then Katrina lunged at me again as if acting out that very thing.

I sidestepped her, taking the brunt of her weight on my shoulder as she slammed us both against the wall.

"You confronted Vlad about killing your sister?" I asked.

"Yes. But the coward denied it."

"So you killed him."

She looked up, eyes still flashing. "He killed my sister! I was entitled to revenge!"

I gulped. Clearly.

"And when I started asking questions, you hit me on the head," I said.

"I just wanted to scare you off. I needed more time"

"Time to get money to leave the country. You were going to sell the last item you had, then take the cash and flee."

"I was." She paused, eyes penetrating me. "I *am*," she corrected.

Before I could stop her she shoved me backward hard enough that I fell on my butt, skidding on my wet skirt along the cold floor. Then she turned and ran, full tilt, toward the glowing red "exit" sign that led outside.

I scrambled to my feet, but as I watched her sprint to the door, I knew I was too far away to catch her. By the time I got there, she'd be gone, disappearing into any one of the waiting taxis, and on her way to any one of a dozen different ways out of the city.

I followed after her, praying she tripped, praying she couldn't catch a cab, praying anything I could think of that involved her not getting away as I watched her slip through the exit, the door shutting with a thud after her.

But for once, someone up there must have been listening.

Because as I pushed through the exit a minute later, I ran right into a huge crowd of paparazzi on the sidewalk with cameras in hand, flashes going off in every direction.

And at the center of it stood Katrina, shielding her eyes at the onslaught.

"I'm not Irina," she protested over the sound of questions being fired at her from every direction.

"Did you fake your death?"

"Are you having an affair with Ricky?"

"Did you set him up to take the fall?"

"Who does your hair?"

"Leave me alone!" Katrina yelled, fighting to make her way to a waiting line of taxis at the curb.

But I was faster this time. I shoved through the crowd and grabbed Katrina by the arm.

"Gotcha," I told her, grinning from ear to ear.

For once, the paparazzi saved the day.

CHAPTER NINETEEN

An hour later I was sitting on a bench at baggage claim, watching the police question Katrina. As soon as I'd had her in hand, I'd flagged down a security officer outside the claim area and told him to call Ramirez with information that his wife had caught an international criminal. I figured that would get his attention. The officer had, and, within minutes, LAPD were swarming the airport. Which had done little to calm the frenzied paparazzi and even less to reassure the crowds of travelers. It would be a miracle if we didn't make the six o'clock news.

Dana had caught up to me about the same time the police had arrived, out of breath and followed by a small band of groupies. Apparently word had spread like wildfire that Dana Dashel was at the Burbank airport, looking fabulous and signing autographs, and all paparazzi within a three freeway radius had descended upon the airport. Luckily for me, right about when Katrina had tried to make a break for it. Then, seeing who they all thought was Irina, the paparazzi had first peed their collective pants, then mobbed her with their cameras. Which is right about when I'd arrived on scene.

For once, I was thrilled with the press. Especially since, as I browsed on my phone, I noticed that Dana was showing up on every tabloid website on the front page... looking absolutely fabulous in her gown. If this didn't make up for the Crocs, I didn't know what did.

"Is he gonna be mad?" Dana asked, sitting on the bench next to me.

I turned in the direction she was indicating: a small office where Ramirez had Katrina handcuffed and awaiting transport to the county jail for processing. My husband hadn't had a chance to do more than glance my way when he'd arrived on scene, instead focusing on Katrina. (Who, by the way was so pissed off at the reporters that she'd been yelling in Russian non-stop.) Fearing the worst, I'd texted Mom and Mrs. R to take the kids home. I didn't want them to have to witness their dad murdering their mom.

I nodded. "Oh, yeah. He's gonna be mad."

"I'm sorry."

"Thanks. But it was inevitable he'd find out sometime. I can only hope he's at least a little grateful that we did help solve his case."

Dana nodded. "Well, even if he isn't grateful, I, for one, am." She gave me a hug that was so fierce it almost cracked a rib. From outside the baggage area, I saw more cameras going off, transmitting the scene to tabloids around the globe.

As if on cue, the door to the small office opened, accompanied by the sound of Russian cursing, mixed with an English expletive here and there. Ramirez emerged, his eyes scanning the room, then narrowing into dark, dangerous slits when he found me.

I gulped, feeling the weight of his stare like a ton of bricks.

"Uh-oh," Dana whispered beside me.

No kidding.

Ramirez made purposeful strides across the room and in an instant was standing right in front of me.

"Maddie." He said my name in a flat monotone that gave no clue to the emotion behind it.

I did a little one-finger wave. "Hi, honey."

The eyes narrowed further.

"Uh, maybe I should just go wait for you over there..." Dana trailed off, sliding from her seat and making for the vending machines in the corner. Outside a mob of photographers followed her, still snapping photos through the windows.

I cleared my throat, shifted from cheek to cheek on my seat, felt my upper lip begin to sweat.

"So, the twin did it, huh?" I asked, my voice high and squeaky with false casualness. "Who knew, right?"

Ramirez crossed his arms over his chest. "Apparently *you* did."

I bit my lip. "Okay, see, here's the thing. I totally didn't mean to investigate behind your back, it just kinda happened. You know, sort of like the way you arrested Ricky behind my back."

"Springer..." he growled in warning.

"But this isn't about what you did," I quickly covered. "It's about what I did. Which was wrong. And I'm sorry. I should have been above board with it all. I shouldn't have lied and snuck around. But you have to understand that Ricky needed me. And I couldn't just sit back and do nothing, so I'm really, really, really sorry that I was investigating on my own, and I'm so sorry you were in the dark about it."

Ramirez stared at me for a long beat. Then he finally said. "Well, I wasn't completely in the dark."

I paused. "Wait, what do you mean?"

Ramirez shot me a look. "Jesus, Maddie, I *am* a detective."

Mental forehead thunk. "So you knew what I was doing all along?"

"I had a suspicion," he confessed, sitting down on the bench beside me.

"Why didn't you say anything? Yell at me? Try to stop me?"

He shrugged. "What would the point have been? You were going to investigate anyway, right?"

"Probably," I confessed.

He cocked his head at me and shot me that look again. "Okay, yes, totally."

"Right. It would have been wasted breath on my part to try to talk you out of it. Besides, I knew you wouldn't do anything to endanger the kids."

"I didn't. They were totally at home when I got this," I assured him, pointing to my nose.

The corner of his mouth quirked upward in the beginnings of a smile. "I was going to ask what happened there. I think your silly putty is falling off."

I turned to catch my reflection in the glass behind me. Sure enough, the mondo-strength cover-up was peeling off in flesh-colored chunks. Fab. And *this* was the face the paparazzi were filming?

"I suck so badly," I told him. "I'm so sorry I lied to you."

"I'm sorry, too. But I get it," he said, nodding. "I should have put more in faith in you from the beginning. I know you're not stupid. If you were in real trouble, you'd call me for help. And, well, in all honesty you're not half bad at solving this sort of stuff."

I blinked. "Could you repeat that?" I asked.

"What?"

"The part about you saying I rock at solving homicides. I'd just like it to go on record. Officially. Maybe even in writing on a plaque to hang above the bed."

He grinned. "Very funny, Springer."

I shook my head. "I never thought this day would come. You're actually condoning me butting into your investigations."

He frowned and held up a hand. "Whoa, let's not go that far. But let's just say that I've learned there are certain times in a marriage when the best thing you can do is keep your mouth shut."

I couldn't help the ear to ear grin that spread across my face. "I couldn't agree more." I grabbed him around the middle, snuggling into the crook of his arm for a long, lingering hug.

"I'm sorry I investigated behind your back. It won't happen again," I said.

I felt Ramirez chuckle, a deep rumble that reverberated way down in his chest. "Yes, it will."

"No, I-" I started to protest.

But he cut me off. "But, I'll forgive you then, too." He popped a kiss on the top of my head. "Just like you forgive me for being a little overprotective at times. I should know by now that you can take care of yourself."

I bit my lip. "Most of the time," I added, feeling bruises from my confrontation with Katrina already forming. I looked up at the office where she was still waving her arms and yelling. "So, is she talking?" I asked, gesturing toward our suspect.

Ramirez nodded. "Oh, yeah. Talking up a storm. Only problem is it's half in Russian. We're getting a translator now."

"She told me she killed Vlad." I paused, watching his eyes for a glint of recognition. "The Russian smuggler in the hotel."

He nodded. "I had a bad feeling that one of those blondes seen at the scene might be mine."

"Sorry." I said "Again."

"We recovered a gun in the dumpster behind the hotel. The serial number was filed off, but CSU did find a partial print. If it's Katrina's, it shouldn't be hard to match."

"Which reminds me, some more evidence should be arriving at our house via overnight shipping soon."

Ramirez shot me a look.

"It's best if you don't ask."

"You're gonna end up creating a whole mountain of paperwork for me, aren't you?"

"Am I wearing out the word 'sorry' at this point?"

He grinned, a full-fledged thing that took over his face. "You're getting there."

"Will it help if I tell you what Katrina confessed to me?"

"It wouldn't hurt."

So, I did, relaying the entire conversation. "Katrina said she killed Vlad because he killed Irina," I ended with.

Ramirez nodded. "That jives with what she's been screaming in there, too. We'll compare the hairs left at the scene to Vlad's. It should be easy to tell if they're a match."

I cut my eyes to the office, where I could see Katrina waving her hands as she shouted about something. I felt a frown burrow between my eyebrows. "You know, there's still just one thing that doesn't make sense to me," I said.

"What's that?"

"How did Vlad get onto the *Dancing with Celebrities* set?" I asked.

Ramirez gave me a blank look. "What do you mean?"

"To kill Irina. He had to get onto the UBN studio lot. And, trust me, it isn't easy to get past that guy at the security guard house."

Ramirez shot me another look.

"Okay, gloss over how I know that. But still, how did he get in?"

My husband shook his head. "I don't know. Maybe he lied to the guard, maybe he had someone bring him on as a guest, maybe Irina let him in."

I felt that frown dig in deeper. "Maybe," I hedged. Though I didn't see any of those scenarios as very likely. Irina and he were already at odds, and she knew it. I didn't see her inviting him in to kill her.

"Anyway," Ramirez said, "with Vlad dead, we probably won't ever know."

A truth that did nothing to alleviate the ridge between my eyebrows.

Ramirez grinned at me again, a lopsided thing that showed off the dimple in his left cheek.

"What?" I asked.

He shrugged. "Nothing. It's just, you're kinda cute when you're all deep in thought like that."

I felt the frown melting away. "Just kinda cute?"

"Pretty dammed cute," he amended

"So, you're not mad at me?" I asked.

Ramirez held up his thumb and forefinger an inch apart. "Just this much."

"Tell you what? I promise I can make it up to you."

"Oh really?" He raised an eyebrow, putting an arm around me. "And how would that be, Springer?"

I shrugged. "I could make lasagna tomorrow night for dinner?"

He nodded, leaning in just that much closer. "That would be nice. But I'm not sure it entirely makes up for lying to me."

"I could follow it up with cake?"

"Ooo," he said, his eyebrows drawing together as his mouth puckered. "I like cake." He paused, moving in closer. "But there's something I like even more than cake."

I felt my knees go weak, my spine melting into the chair as he leaned in so close his lips were just inches from mine.

"Oh yeah?" I asked. "And what would that be?"

Ramirez's eyes went dark and dangerous, melting into two pools of delicious chocolate. "Guess," he whispered. Then he kissed me.

Oh, boy, did he kiss me.

* * *

It was a miracle. The twins actually slept a full six hours each that night, and even five of those were at the same time. I woke up feeling like a new person. Granted, it was a bit of a sore person, the fight with Katrina having taken its toll on me, but I only required two strong cups of coffee to get my brain into gear.

I quickly showered and dressed and checked my phone messages. I had twenty texts and half a dozen voicemails. Three were from Mom in various states of excitement as she saw my face on not only the six o'clock news, but also the ten o'clock and eleven o'clock versions as well.

One voicemail was dated this morning from Dana saying she was going to the courthouse to pick up Ricky, as he was officially released.

Ramirez texted saying he was processing Katrina today, but would be home for lasagna come hell or high water.

Marco texted to say *ohmigod u ok dahling?* and that he was spending the day with his new BFF, Ling, helping her plan a birthday party to end all birthday parties.

And, after deleting them all, I decided I was going to spend some serious quality *Dora the Explorer* time with my babies today.

But, I just had one little thing I wanted to do first.

While I was pretty sure Lana had seen the news this morning telling her just who had been stealing her wardrobe items, I felt I owed it to my old friend to give her the details in person. (And, there was the issue of the gorgeous blue scarf I'd seen in her shop. Call me crazy, but it seemed like the perfect we-solved-the-case splurge.)

I texted Mom to come watch the twins, which was she was only too happy to do. In fact, she was so happy that as soon as she arrived her cooing and gurgling at the twins was infectious, instantly transforming them from pooping monsters into little laughing angels. I watched the trio doing baby-talk at each other, perfectly content to tune me out.

"Okay, I give up. What's the trick?" I asked Mom.

Mom blinked at me. "Trick?"

"How do you *do* that? Make them immediately stop crying? Are you doing some baby-whisperer thing? Do you slip them Prozac? What?"

Mom smiled, her eyes crinkling at the corners. "Oh, honey. There's no trick."

"Then what am I doing wrong?" I asked, throwing my hands in the air.

Mom put an arm around me. "You're not doing anything wrong. You're a new mother. You haven't slept, you're tired, and you're overwhelmed."

"Yes, yes, and yes," I agreed.

"On the other hand," Mom went on, "I get to swoop in, be fun grandma for a couple of hours, then go home and recuperate. It's easy to be the baby whisperer when you're only on duty in short shifts."

"That's it?" I asked, relief washing over me. "You mean, they don't prefer you to me?"

Mom grinned. "Honey, you just need a break from each other every now and then. Trust me, if they had to be with me all the time, they'd be wailing bloody murder."

I looked down at Livvie and Max. Their little dark eyes blinked innocently up at me.

"They do love it when you visit though," I told Mom.

"I love it, too."

"Okay, I have a proposal to make," I decided.

Mom raised an eyebrow at me. "A proposal?"

"Since they seem to enjoy the break with Grandma so much. In small doses," I added. "How would you like to come watch them on a regular basis. Say, a couple of hours every morning while I get back to designing?"

Mom's eyes lit up. "Oh, that would be wonderful!" She clapped her hands. "You hear that babies, Grandma's gonna be your babysitter," she told them.

Max and Livvie cooed back, and I swear I even saw Max start to giggle with delight.

I'll admit, I felt a little delighted too. The idea of actually designing again was exciting. And knowing that the little break from each other was good for all of us meant I could do it guilt-free.

Pleased with the new arrangement, I left Mom and the babies making little googly faces at each other as I hopped into my minivan and hit traffic.

I parked my car in the garage on Melrose, walked the two blocks to The Sunshine State, and pushed through the front doors, hearing the little bell chime above the door.

And the first thing I saw was Allie Quick. What's worse, she was purchasing *my* blue scarf from the pink-haired girl at the register.

I narrowed my eyes.

"Allie," I said.

She spun around at the sound of my voice. "Maddie."

We stood there staring at each other in a silent standoff, each daring the other to start first.

Finally I cracked.

"Nice scarf," I managed.

Allie looked down at her bag. "Oh. Yeah, I saw this super cute thing last time I was here, and I just had to come back and get it."

I hated how much we were alike in that moment.

Allie pursed her lips, smearing her pale pink lipstick. "So, did you see the story I printed about Dana and Ricky this morning?"

Honestly? In all that had happened, checking the *Informer* website had been low on my priority list. I shook my head in the negative. "What did it say?" I asked, dread building in my gut.

"It said that you and Dana cracked the case wide open. That you single-handedly caught Irina's killer. And that Ricky was innocent all along." She paused. "And there were some really cute pics of Dana in that silver gown."

I bit my lip. Okay, maybe Allie wasn't *all* bad. "Thanks," I said. "She could use the good press right now."

Allie looked down at her feet. "Look, I know you hate me."

I opened my mouth to protest, but she ran right over me.

"It's okay. I get it. I've got big boobs, a not terribly low I.Q., and I'm damned good at my job. A lot of people hate me," she said, an emotion flitting behind her eyes that told me she wasn't as okay with the fact as she was trying to pretend to be. "But honestly? I kind of admire you, Maddie."

"Me?" I said, not able to keep the surprise out of my voice.

She nodded. "Yeah. I mean, you've got a great guy, a great career, two great kids." She paused and did a lopsided grin. "Plus you have this uncanny knack for ferreting out the truth. It's not many women that have it all like you do."

Wow. She thought I had it all. I didn't burst her bubble that I'd spent the better part of the last two weeks with at least half of that "all" hanging by a tenuous thread. My babies were overwhelming, I almost never slept, my husband was gone more often than not, and my career had been on hold for so many months now that I feared I might not remember how to hold a sketching pencil.

But instead of setting her straight, I just said, "Thanks."

"You're welcome."

For once she looked so sincere, that I couldn't stop myself before words started tumbling from my mouth. "Hey, Ricky's going home today. How about I try to set up that interview for you with him tomorrow?"

"Really?" Allie's eyes lit up like a tween at a Justin Bieber concert. "Ohmigod, that would be, like, totally awesome."

I couldn't help grinning back. "Cool. I'll call you tomorrow with the details," I promised.

"You're the best, Maddie!" she called after me, practically skipping out of the store.

I watched her, wondering if maybe I'd judged Allie a little too harshly. I mean, she did have great taste in clothes. Maybe there was hope for her after all.

"Maddie!"

I turned to see Lana emerging from the back room. She was dressed today in a pair of flowing, wrap pants in a tribal print, a long-sleeved shirt in sheer nude that looked amazing against her pale skin, and the same pair of heavy, wooden clogs I'd seen on her the last time I'd been in. "Hi, Lana."

"I heard all about you on the news last night. Are you okay?"

I nodded. "I am. Mostly," I amended, my hand unconsciously going to my nose where the skin was just starting to grow in again. "Thanks for asking."

"So it's all true. That horrible smuggler guy killed Irina?" she asked me.

I nodded, filling her in on all the gory details, including how her wardrobe items had gone missing.

When I finished, she was shaking her head, her black curls bouncing along her shoulders. "Wow. I never would have thought Irina would do such a thing."

"I guess anyone can get a little crazy in a desperate situation," I said.

"Well thank God it's all cleared up now," Lana said. "Hopefully we can all get on with our lives. The show must go on. And the actors must look fabulous, right?" she said, giving me a wink.

"Speaking of fabulous," I said. "I was wondering if you happen to have any more of those blue, silk scarves?" I asked, pointing to the counter where Allie had swiped the last one.

"I might have another in the back," Lana told me. "Tell you what: for clearing up the whole mystery of the missing wardrobe, it's on the house."

"Oh, I couldn't," I protested. Though, I'll admit, I didn't protest very hard. With the amount I'd shelled out on eBay for shoes that were now evidence, my bank account was starting to squeak again.

"I insist," Lana said. "Just wait here a minute, and I'll be right back."

She turned and made for the back room, her wooden clogs clomping on the tile floor as she did.

And that's when I saw it.

I froze, my entire body going stiff as I watched Lana lift one foot then the other, toward the back room. On the back of the custom, one-of-a-kind shoes that she'd designed, carved into the heel, was a distinct crosshatch pattern in a triangle shape.

Just like the weapon that had killed Irina.

CHAPTER TWENTY

———

I looked from Lana's retreating back to the pink-haired girl on duty at the counter to the front doors and the deceptively optimistic sunshine beyond. I was completely frozen to the spot, my mind going a million miles a minute, trying to decide what to do.

Finally I pulled out my cell and dialed Ramirez, my fingers trembling as I punched the buttons. It rang on the other end, then again. "Please pick up," I chanted. Prompting the pink-haired girl to turn my way. I gave her what I'm sure was the most forced smile ever and turned away, retreating to the far side of the store, behind a rack of summer shawls.

Four rings in, the call bounced to voicemail. I hung up, dialed again, and listened to it ring four more times before hitting voicemail again.

"It's me," I whispered into the phone. "I know this is going to sound crazy, but Vlad did not kill Irina. I know who did. And I have the murder weapon." I paused. "Well, at least, I know what the murder weapon was and where it is, and I'm pretty sure I know who used it now. It was-"

"Hang up, Maddie."

I froze, feeling something hard and cold suddenly pressing up against my rib cage. I glanced down, and fear lodged in my throat as I saw the barrel of a small, shiny handgun, tickling my side. My gaze traveled slowly upward to a hand, a sheer, nude sleeve, and a mass of black curls, framing the now pale, pinched face of my former friend.

I swallowed hard. Then I did as instructed, hitting the end button on the phone.

"Amy," Lana called over her shoulder to the pink-haired girl. "Why don't you take your break now. I'll watch the counter for a bit."

My eyes darted to the girl, blissfully unaware of what her employer was holding behind the clothing rack.

"'K," Amy said, then grabbed a purse from beneath the counter and headed for the front door.

I silently pleaded with her to turn around, notice what was going on, run for help, call the police, anything!

But Amy walked out the front door, popped a piece of gum into her mouth and strolled toward the parking garage.

I thought a really bad word, feeling my hope slip away with her.

"Now, lock the door," Lana said, her voice a flat monotone. Gone was the happy-go-lucky woman of a moment ago, and in her place was a stone poker face that left no hint of any emotion behind it.

"Lana, don't do this," I said, hearing my voice come out as a shaky whisper. "Please. How long have we known each other?"

Her eyes softened some, though I noticed her grip on the gun was still firm. "I'm sorry, Maddie," she said, "but I have no choice." She gestured toward the glass at the front of the shop. "The door," she prompted again.

I slowly inched in the direction she indicated. "Why?" I asked, my eyes cutting to the street outside the glass. If I could just get someone's attention outside, maybe they could call for help. "Why did you do it?"

"Why?" she repeated. "The same reason I do anything. For fashion," she said, her chin lifting. "Fashion is my life."

"I don't understand," I prompted.

"I have sacrificed everything to get where I am," she said, the words coming out in a rapid stream. "Everything, you understand? No family, no life outside of the studios and the shop. How many times have we gone out since we graduated?"

"Uh, none?" I said, truthfully.

"Exactly! I have nothing but fashion." Her eyes blazed, suddenly taking on a feverish look. "And *she* was going to take that away from me."

"'She,' meaning Irina?" I made it to the door and scanned the street beyond. There was a coffee shop across from us where a couple was sitting outside, drinking from steaming paper cups. Next to that was a jewelry store. On either side of us were other clothing boutiques. A woman with a small dog in her purse entered the one on the left, a teenager wearing earbuds exiting the one on the right. But none of them was paying attention to what was going on inside The Sunshine State.

"Yes, Irina!" Lana spat out, drawing my attention back to her. "She was going to ruin everything. Don't you see, I couldn't have that?"

I nodded, figuring it was better to agree than not when being held at gunpoint.

"Turn the lock," Lana said, indicating a metal catch on the glass door.

I did, hearing my own fate seal with the click.

"Now step away." She waved the gun toward a rack of wide-leg pants just outside the window's line of sight.

I slowly stepped to the left, my eyes scanning the window again for any last hope. The couple outside the coffee shop tossed their cups into the trash and left. A woman with grey hair emerged from the store beside us, walking right past the window. I bit down the urge to wave my hands and madly signal for help as she turned her back to me.

No one was paying attention. Which meant I had to stall, keep Lana talking. Keep her engaged until I could somehow signal for help.

"Irina was the star of your show," I said. "Why kill her?"

Lana shook her head. "Don't you understand Maddie? She was ruining me. The producers thought I was being careless with wardrobe items. They blamed me!"

"And then when the story of the missing pieces leaked to the *Informer*, the press blamed you, too."

"Yes!" she said, nodding. "She was going to kill my career. Everything I had worked for had led up to this point. This show was everything. I was in the running for a costuming Emmy with this show. But after that damned gown of

Shaniqua's went missing, the producers were furious. They were talking about replacing me!"

"I didn't know that," I told her honestly.

Lana nodded, her curls bouncing wildly. "Oh, they were. I heard the rumblings. I had to do something. I was desperate."

"And desperate people do crazy things," I said, repeating the all-too true statement from earlier.

"I didn't mean to," she said, almost as if she were pleading with me to understand. "I really didn't. But when I saw her there that day, I knew what she was doing. It all suddenly clicked."

"You saw her in Ricky's dressing room," I said, the pieces clicking finally for me, too.

Lana nodded. "I was bringing him his waltz outfit to try on for next week. I was just going to hang it in his closet, but when I opened the door to his dressing room, I saw Irina. She was stripping off her red dress and shoving it into a bag. *Her* bag," she emphasized.

"And that's when you realized she was stealing it."

Lana nodded again, her eyes starting to tear. "She was hiding it in the back of Ricky's closet. She wasn't stupid. She knew her dressing room was the first place anyone would look for it, but if she hid it in his room, she could come back for it at the end of the day and easily smuggle it off set."

I nodded, remembering what Kaylie had told me about seeing Irina sneak into Ricky's dressing room before that. Had it been to hide the shoes her sister had sold me?

"Did you confront her?" I asked.

"Of course. I flat out asked her what she was doing."

"And what did she say?" I asked, one eye on the windows. The street was oddly empty now. The one time I was dying for foot traffic, shoppers were totally absent. I felt desperation start to bubble in my throat. I could only keep Lana talking for so long. I was running out of time.

"She denied it at first," Lana said. "But I'd caught her red-handed and she knew it. Finally she confessed. Said it was her taking wardrobe items all along, then selling them. That she needed the money." Lana laughed, a short bark of a thing. "Can you believe the nerve? She was ruining my career and wanted *my* sympathy?"

"Shocking," I agreed. Not that I cared at that point. What I cared about was more time. My eyes scanned the room for anything I could use as a weapon. Skirts, dresses, pants. All flowy and blousy, annoyingly loose and soft. Not even a belt in sight!

"I told her she had to stop," Lana continued. "That I was going to the producers."

"And what did she say?"

She shook her head, an almost sad look in her eyes. "She laughed at me. She said she'd deny it. Who would they believe: the show's star or some 'little wardrobe woman.'"

"And that's when you killed her," I said slowly.

Lana's eyes turned on me, flashing fire again. "I had no choice! She was going to ruin me. She was taking away all I had worked for."

"So you took off your heavy shoe and hit her with it." Death by ugly clog. No matter what she'd done, I had to feel some measure of sympathy for Irina about that.

"I didn't mean to kill her," Lana said, shaking her head again. "I just wanted her to stop. If she had only put the damned dress back on and promised to stop stealing, I wouldn't have had to do anything."

"That's why Irina was found naked," I said, putting it together. "You caught her in the middle of changing. Ricky was telling the truth all along."

"I honestly didn't mean to create trouble for Ricky," she said. "But when the police starting thinking he did it, well, you see why I had to let them think that."

"Which is why you told me you saw Ricky going into the dressing room."

"And I did!" Lana protested. She paused. "Just not right before Irina died. It was earlier. I saw him leave first. Then I went in."

"He could have gone to jail," I told her, unable to keep the edge of anger on my friend's behalf out of my voice.

Lana's curls bounced as she shook her head again. "No. He has money. He's famous. His lawyer would have gotten him off."

"And you would have gotten away with it."

"I *will* get away with it," Lana said slowly. "There was no way I was letting Irina derail all I had worked for." She paused, her head cocking to the side, sadness returning to her eyes. "And I'm sorry, but there's no way I'm letting you either, Maddie."

Uh-oh.

I gulped, feeling a lump form in my throat. "You don't have to do this, Lana. You can turn yourself in."

"Ha!" she laughed, though there was zero joy in the sound. "And what? Spend twenty-to-life in San Quentin? No thanks, Maddie."

"Please, Lana, don't do this," I pleaded, hearing the fear in my own voice. My eyes whipped wildly to the right and left. No one was outside, there was nothing I could use as a weapon within reach, and that gun was held steady in her hand, trained right on my torso, her finger gripping the trigger tightly.

"I'm sorry, Maddie," she said, her voice holding a note of actual regret. "I'm so sorry it has to be this way."

"You won't get away with it," I told her, switching tactics. "Too many people know I'm here. They know I came to see you. They'll find me and arrest you."

Lana nodded. "Oh they will find you. Shot dead on the floor. The register will be empty, the window broken, and I'll be in the back, looking like I've been beaten up. A robbery gone wrong," she said. "A horrible tragedy."

I swallowed. Damned. She's really thought this through. Kudos to her for thinking on her feet.

I, on the other hand, was drawing a blank on mine. In fact, all I could think of was that despite my love of shopping in life, the last place I wanted to die was a trendy boutique on Melrose.

I watched Lana take a step closer, gun straight-armed in front of her. Her eyes clouded over with tears, but her aim never waivered.

I bit my lip. I felt my insides turn to jelly, my breath come fast, my fight or flight response kicking in overtime. But I couldn't think of a single way to either fight or flee that didn't involve Lana pulling the trigger before I could do more than move an inch.

I felt warm tears on my face as visions of Ramirez, my Mom, Dana, and my sweet little babies flashed through my mind like a slideshow.

"I'm sorry." I saw Lana mouth the words as her finger closed in around the trigger.

I closed my eyes, cringing as I braced for the hot burn of a bullet.

Then I heard it. The shot echoed in the small boutique, the sound ringing in my ears, accompanied by glass shattering in every direction, spraying my back and shoulders with dozens of tiny shards.

I held my breath. And it took me a second to realize I *had* breath. I was still alive.

I slowly blinked my eyes back open.

Then stifled a gasp as I saw Lana sprawled out on the floor in front of me, a tiny, red hole in the center of her chest, sticky liquid quickly spreading across her sheer top.

I whipped my head around, eyes focusing on a figure standing on the sidewalk, just outside the now shattered window.

Blonde hair, D-cups almost spilling from her tight tank, mini skirt riding high on her tanned thighs, and the cutest pink gun you ever saw held in a pair of manicured hands, the tip smoking in the sunshine, still aimed right at the spot where Lana had been.

Allie blinked at me, seemingly almost as shocked at what had just happened as I was.

"You okay?" she asked, her voice shaky.

I nodded. "Nice timing, Quick."

The corner of her mouth quirked upward. "The scarf still had the security tag on it. I was bringing it back when I saw the gun in the window. Didn't take a genius to figure out you needed backup."

Allie might be perky enough to annoy a hummingbird, but I'd take her kind of back-up any day.

CHAPTER TWENTY-ONE

"What was it like knowing that everyone thought you were guilty?" Allie Quick leaned in, her eyes intent on Ricky as she asked the question.

Ricky cheated his face toward the camera over Allie's left shoulder like a pro, making sure the light hit his jaw at just the right angle before he answered.

"It was rough, I'm not going to lie," he told her.

"But through it all, one person believed in you, didn't she?" Allie prompted.

Ricky nodded, his eyes turning to the chair beside him where Dana sat, holding his hand. "Yes, she did. Dana's my rock," he said.

Dana smiled at him, squeezing his hand a little tighter.

"And how long have you two been dating now?" Tina Bender cut in, sitting in a chair just beside Allie.

While I'd made the promised call to set up the interview with Ricky for Allie (Hey, she had saved my life after all.), I *had* promised an interview to Tina as well. After listening to the two paparazzo's fight it out over who got the interview first, Ricky finally proposed that they could interview him in tandem. As much as Allie wasn't 100% thrilled with sharing, Felix had been ecstatic that the *Informer* would be the only tabloid in town with the exclusive.

I watched the two women jockey for alpha-dog position in the interview from my chair just outside of camera range. I silently sipped my venti mocha Frappuccino as I waited for Dana's answer. (If almost getting shot had taught me anything, it was that life was way too short to spend it dieting.)

"We've been together for three years," Dana replied.

"And there's never been anyone but her in those three years," Ricky cut in. He turned to Dana. "I mean, look at her. Why would I ever want anyone else?"

Dana blushed, the color of her cheeks perfectly complementing her Lover Girl passion pink lipstick.

"There's still one thing our readers would like to know," Allie said, taking over the interview again. "Ricky, you refused to give an alibi when you were arrested. Why?"

I bit my lip. Honestly? I kind of wanted to know that, too. All along I'd had the feeling Ricky was hiding something. While I'd been sure it was cheating on Dana at the time, Lana's version of events had backed up Ricky's story completely. So, if he hadn't been cheating on her, what had he been hiding from Dana?

Ricky took a deep breath, his eyes cutting to Dana as he let go of her hand. "Right. My alibi. Well, I wasn't lying when I said I was on the UBN lot at the time."

Dana sighed in relief.

"But I was lying when I said I was alone."

The relief disappeared in a flash. I saw Dana suck in a breath, her spine straighten, her hands clench in her lap.

"I was actually meeting with someone else," Ricky confessed. "Someone I didn't want anyone to know about."

Dana began breathing hard. I chewed my lip and prepared to pull her off of him if need be.

Allie and Tina leaned forward as one, practically salivating.

"And that person was?" Tina asked.

Ricky took a deep breath. "Neil Lane."

Allie's brow puckered, mirroring the collective curiosity in the room. "Wait - the jewelry designer?"

Ricky nodded. Then he reached into the breast pocket of his jacket and pulled out a small, velvet-covered box.

I sucked in a breath, recognizing the size and shape immediately.

Dana gasped, hands flying to her mouth.

Allie and Tina practically vibrated with excitement in their seats as Ricky knelt down on the floor, still careful to keep his face cheated toward the camera, and took Dana's left hand in his.

"I am so sorry for any pain I put you through," he started, his eyes sincere and intent on hers. "You mean the world to me, and I would never intentionally hurt you."

Dana swallowed hard, nodding. "Uh-huh?" she prompted.

"You are everything I've ever wanted in a woman. Kind, smart, sweet, beautiful inside and out," he continued.

"Uh-huh, uh-huh," Dana said, nodding, her eyes intent on the velvet box.

"All my life I've been searching for someone like you, and I can't imagine what I ever did to deserve a woman as kind and smart and sweet and-"

"I love you, too," Dana said, cutting him off. "But for the love of God, open that box!"

Ricky grinned. "Did I mention how much I love your feistiness, too?"

Dana bit her lip, the anticipation coming off of her in waves.

Ricky cleared his throat. "Okay, here goes." He flipped open the lid on the velvet box, exposing a diamond so bright I suddenly needed sunglasses. "Dana Dashel, will you do me the honor of becoming my wife-"

"Yes!" Dana cried, jumping up from her seat and throwing her arms around Ricky's neck with such force that it knocked him backward into his chair again.

Ricky and Dana engaged in a lip lock that I'm sure was going to be tweeted a million times before the end of the day. Allie and Tina gave each other a high-five and did a couple of fist bumps at breaking the celebrity news of the year.

And I couldn't help the ear-to-ear grin on my face.

My babies were safe at home with their loving grandmother, my husband was hard at work making the streets of L.A. safe for us all, I was slowly getting back to doing what I loved in the fashion world, the tabloids were printing *good* news for a change, and my best friend was now wearing a custom designed rock the size of a golf ball. Life was good.

And pretty soon, if we didn't watch out, Dana and I were going to be a pair of old, married women.

Of course, that didn't mean we couldn't still get into just a *little* trouble now and then.

ABOUT THE AUTHOR

Gemma Halliday is the *New York Times* and *USA* Today bestselling author of the *High Heels Mysteries*, the *Hollywood Headlines Mysteries,* and the *Deadly Cool* series of young adult books, as well as several other works. Gemma's books have received numerous awards, including a Golden Heart, a National Reader's Choice award and three RITA nominations. She currently lives in the San Francisco Bay Area where she is hard at work on several new projects.

To learn more about Gemma, visit her online at www.GemmaHalliday.com

CPSIA information can be obtained at www.ICGtesting.com
Printed in the USA
LVOW081640230613

339843LV00001B/111/P